PENGUIN POPULAR CLASSICS

HENRY V

WILLIAM
SHAKESPEARE

PENGUIN BOOKS

PENGUIN BOOKS

Published by the Penguin Group
Penguin Books Ltd, 27 Wrights Lane, London W8 5TZ, England
Penguin Putnam Inc., 375 Hudson Street, New York, New York 10014, USA
Penguin Books Australia Ltd, Ringwood, Victoria, Australia
Penguin Books Canada Ltd, 10 Alcorn Avenue, Toronto, Ontario, Canada M4V 3B2
Penguin Books (NZ) Ltd, Private Bag 102902, NSMC, Auckland, New Zealand

Penguin Books Ltd, Registered Offices: Harmondsworth, Middlesex, England

Published in Penguin Popular Classics 1994
5 7 9 10 8 6 4

Printed in England by Cox & Wyman Ltd, Reading, Berkshire

PENGUIN POPULAR CLASSICS

HENRY V

BY WILLIAM SHAKESPEARE

CONTENTS

The Works of Shakespeare 6

William Shakespeare 7

The Elizabethan Theatre 11

The Life of Henry the Fifth (Introduction) 15

THE LIFE OF HENRY THE FIFTH 21

Notes 130

Glossary 141

THE WORKS OF SHAKESPEARE

PLAYS

APPROXIMATE DATE		FIRST PRINTED
Before 1594	HENRY VI *three parts*	*Folio* 1623
	RICHARD III	1597
	TITUS ANDRONICUS	1594
	LOVE'S LABOUR'S LOST	1598
	THE TWO GENTLEMEN OF VERONA	*Folio*
	THE COMEDY OF ERRORS	*Folio*
	THE TAMING OF THE SHREW	*Folio*
1594–1597	ROMEO AND JULIET (*pirated* 1597)	1599
	A MIDSUMMER NIGHT'S DREAM	1600
	RICHARD II	1597
	KING JOHN	*Folio*
	THE MERCHANT OF VENICE	1600
1597–1600	HENRY IV *part i*	1598
	HENRY IV *part ii*	1600
	HENRY V (*pirated* 1600)	*Folio*
	MUCH ADO ABOUT NOTHING	1600
	MERRY WIVES OF WINDSOR (*pirated* 1602)	*Folio*
	AS YOU LIKE IT	*Folio*
	JULIUS CAESAR	*Folio*
	TROYLUS AND CRESSIDA	1609
1601–1608	HAMLET (*pirated* 1603)	1604
	TWELFTH NIGHT	*Folio*
	MEASURE FOR MEASURE	*Folio*
	ALL'S WELL THAT ENDS WELL	*Folio*
	OTHELLO	1622
	LEAR	1608
	MACBETH	*Folio*
	TIMON OF ATHENS	*Folio*
	ANTONY AND CLEOPATRA	*Folio*
	CORIOLANUS	*Folio*
After 1608	PERICLES (*omitted from the Folio*)	1609
	CYMBELINE	*Folio*
	THE WINTER'S TALE	*Folio*
	THE TEMPEST	*Folio*
	HENRY VIII	*Folio*

POEMS

DATES UNKNOWN	VENUS AND ADONIS	1593
	THE RAPE OF LUCRECE	1594
	SONNETS A LOVER'S COMPLAINT	1609
	THE PHOENIX AND THE TURTLE	1601

WILLIAM SHAKESPEARE

William Shakespeare was born at Stratford upon Avon in April, 1564. He was the third child, and eldest son, of John Shakespeare and Mary Arden. His father was one of the most prosperous men of Stratford, who held in turn the chief offices in the town. His mother was of gentle birth, the daughter of Robert Arden of Wilmcote. In December, 1582, Shakespeare married Ann Hathaway, daughter of a farmer of Shottery, near Stratford; their first child Susanna was baptized on May 6, 1583, and twins, Hamnet and Judith, on February 22, 1585. Little is known of Shakespeare's early life; but it is unlikely that a writer who dramatized such an incomparable range and variety of human kinds and experiences should have spent his early manhood entirely in placid pursuits in a country town. There is one tradition, not universally accepted, that he fled from Stratford because he was in trouble for deer stealing, and had fallen foul of Sir Thomas Lucy, the local magnate; another that he was for some time a schoolmaster.

From 1592 onwards the records are much fuller. In March, 1592, the Lord Strange's players produced a new play at the Rose Theatre called *Harry the Sixth*, which was very successful, and was probably the *First Part of Henry VI*. In the autumn of 1592 Robert Greene, the best known of the professional writers, as he was dying wrote a letter to three fellow writers in which he warned them against the ingratitude of players in general, and in particular against an 'upstart crow' who 'supposes he is as much able to bombast out a blank verse as the best of you: and being an absolute Johannes Factotum is in his own conceit the only

Shake-scene in a country.' This is the first reference to Shakespeare, and the whole passage suggests that Shakespeare had become suddenly famous as a playwright. At this time Shakespeare was brought into touch with Edward Alleyne the great tragedian, and Christopher Marlowe, whose thundering parts of Tamburlaine, the Jew of Malta and Dr Faustus Alleyne was acting, as well as Hieronimo, the hero of Kyd's *Spanish Tragedy*, the most famous of all Elizabethan plays.

In April, 1593, Shakespeare published his poem *Venus and Adonis*, which was dedicated to the young Earl of Southampton: it was a great and lasting success, and was reprinted nine times in the next few years. In May, 1594, his second poem, *The Rape of Lucrece*, was also dedicated to Southampton.

There was little playing in 1593, for the theatres were shut during a severe outbreak of the plague; but in the autumn of 1594, when the plague ceased, the playing companies were re-organized, and Shakespeare became a sharer in the Lord Chamberlain's company who went to play in the Theatre in Shoreditch. During these months Marlowe and Kyd had died. Shakespeare was thus for a time without a rival. He had already written the three parts of *Henry VI*, *Richard III*, *Titus Andronicus*, *Two Gentlemen of Verona*, *Love's Labour's Lost*, *The Comedy of Errors*, and *The Taming of the Shrew*. Soon afterwards he wrote the first of his greater plays – *Romeo and Juliet* – and he followed this success in the next three years with *A Midsummer Night's Dream*, *Richard II* and *The Merchant of Venice*. The two parts of *Henry IV*, introducing Falstaff, the most popular of all his comic characters, were written in 1597–8.

The company left the Theatre in 1597 owing to disputes over a renewal of the ground lease, and went to play at the

Curtain in the same neighbourhood. The disputes continued throughout 1598, and at Christmas the players settled the matter by demolishing the old Theatre and re-erecting a new playhouse on the South bank of the Thames, near Southwark Cathedral. This playhouse was named the Globe. The expenses of the new building were shared by the chief members of the Company, including Shakespeare, who was now a man of some means. In 1596 he had bought New Place, a large house in the centre of Stratford, for £60, and through his father purchased a coat-of-arms from the Heralds, which was the official recognition that he and his family were gentlefolk.

By the summer of 1598 Shakespeare was recognized as the greatest of English dramatists. Booksellers were printing his more popular plays, at times even in pirated or stolen versions, and he received a remarkable tribute from a young writer named Francis Meres, in his book *Palladis Tamia*. In a long catalogue of English authors Meres gave Shakespeare more prominence than any other writer, and mentioned by name twelve of his plays.

Shortly before the Globe was opened, Shakespeare had completed the cycle of plays dealing with the whole story of the Wars of the Roses with *Henry V*. It was followed by *As You Like it*, and *Julius Caesar*, the first of the maturer tragedies. In the next three years he wrote *Troylus and Cressida*, *The Merry Wives of Windsor*, *Hamlet* and *Twelfth Night*.

On March 24, 1603, Queen Elizabeth died. The company had often performed before her, but they found her successor a far more enthusiastic patron. One of the first acts of King James was to take over the company and to promote them to be his own servants so that henceforward they were known as the King's Men. They acted now very frequently at Court, and prospered accordingly. In the early years of the reign Shakespeare wrote the more sombre comedies, *All's Well that Ends Well*, and *Measure for Measure*, which were followed by *Othello, Macbeth* and *King Lear*. Then he returned to Roman themes with *Antony and Cleopatra* and *Coriolanus*.

Since 1601 Shakespeare had been writing less, and there were now a number of rival dramatists who were introducing new styles of drama, particularly Ben Jonson (whose first successful comedy, *Every Man in his Humour*, was acted by Shakespeare's company in 1598), Chapman, Dekker, Marston, and Beaumont and Fletcher who began to write in 1607. In 1608 the King's Men acquired a second playhouse, an indoor private theatre in the fashionable quarter of the Blackfriars. At private theatres, plays were performed indoors; the prices charged were higher than in the public playhouses, and the audience consequently was more select. Shakespeare seems to have retired from the stage about this time: his name does not occur in the various lists of players after 1607. Henceforward he lived for the most part at Stratford, where he was regarded as one of the most important citizens. He still wrote a few plays, and he tried his hand at the new form of tragi-comedy – a play with tragic incidents but a happy ending – which Beaumont and Fletcher had popularized. He wrote four of these – *Pericles, Cymbeline, The Winter's Tale* and *The Tempest*, which was acted at Court in 1611. For the last four years of his life he lived in retirement. His son Hamnet had died in 1596: his two daughters were now married. Shakespeare died at Stratford upon Avon on April 23, 1616, and was buried in the chancel of the church, before the high altar. Shortly afterwards a memorial which still exists, with a portrait bust, was set up on the North wall. His wife survived him.

When Shakespeare died fourteen of his plays had been separately published in Quarto booklets. In 1623 his surviving fellow actors, John Heming and Henry Condell, with the co-operation of a number of printers, published a collected edition of thirty-six plays in one Folio volume, with an engraved portrait, memorial verses by Ben Jonson and others, and an Epistle to the Reader in which Heming and Condell make the interesting note that Shakespeare's 'hand and mind went together, and what he thought, he uttered with that easiness that we have scarce received from him a blot in his papers.'

The plays as printed in the Quartos or the Folio differ considerably from the usual modern text. They are often not divided into scenes, and sometimes not even into acts. Nor are there place-headings at the beginning of each scene, because in the Elizabethan theatre there was no scenery. They are carelessly printed and the spelling is erratic.

THE ELIZABETHAN THEATRE

Although plays of one sort and another had been acted for many generations, no permanent playhouse was erected in England until 1576. In the 1570's the Lord Mayor and Aldermen of the City of London and the players were constantly at variance. As a result James Burbage, then the leader of the great Earl of Leicester's players, decided that he would erect a playhouse outside the jurisdiction of the Lord Mayor, where the players would no longer be hindered by the authorities. Accordingly in 1576 he built the Theatre in Shoreditch, at that time a suburb of London The experiment was successful, and by 1592 there were two more playhouses in London, the Curtain (also in Shoreditch), and the Rose on the south bank of the river, near Southwark Cathedral.

Elizabethan players were accustomed to act on a variety of stages; in the great hall of a nobleman's house, or one of the Queen's palaces, in town halls and in yards, as well as their own theatre.

The public playhouse for which most of Shakespeare's plays were written was a small and intimate affair. The outside measurement of the Fortune Theatre, which was built in 1600 to rival the new Globe, was but eighty feet square. Playhouses were usually circular or hexagonal, with three tiers of galleries looking down upon the yard or pit, which was open to the sky. The stage jutted out into the yard so that the actors came forward into the midst of their audience.

Over the stage there was a roof, and on either side doors by which the characters entered or disappeared. Over the back of the stage ran a gallery or upper stage which was used whenever an upper scene was needed, as when Romeo climbs up to Juliet's bedroom, or the citizens of Angiers address King John from the walls. The space beneath this upper stage was known as the tiring house; it was concealed from the audience by a curtain which would be drawn back to reveal an inner stage, for such scenes as the witches' cave in Macbeth, Prospero's cell or Juliet's tomb.

There was no general curtain concealing the whole stage, so that all scenes on the main stage began with an entrance and ended with an exit. Thus in tragedies the dead must be carried away. There was no scenery, and therefore no limit to the number of scenes, for a scene came to an end when the characters left the stage. When it was necessary for the exact locality of a scene to be known, then Shakespeare

THE GLOBE THEATRE

Wood-engraving by R. J. Beedham after a reconstruction by J. C. Adams

indicated it in the dialogue; otherwise a simple property or a garment was sufficient; a chair or stool showed an indoor scene, a man wearing riding boots was a messenger, a king wearing armour was on the battlefield, or the like. Such simplicity was on the whole an advantage; the spectator was not distracted by the setting and Shakespeare was able to use as many scenes as he wished. The action passed by very quickly; a play of 2500 lines of verse could be acted in two hours. Moreover, since the actor was so close to his audience, the slightest subtlety of voice and gesture was easily appreciated.

The company was a 'Fellowship of Players', who were all partners and sharers. There were usually ten to fifteen full members, with three or four boys, and some paid servants. Shakespeare had therefore to write for his team. The chief actor in the company was Richard Burbage, who first distinguished himself as Richard III; for him Shakespeare wrote his great tragic parts. An important member of the company was the clown or low comedian. From 1594 to 1600 the company's clown was Will Kemp; he was succeeded by Robert Armin. No women were allowed to appear on the stage, and all women's parts were taken by boys.

THE LIFE OF HENRY THE FIFTH

The Life of Henry the Fifth was first staged in the spring of 1599. It can be dated with some precision, for in the Chorus before Act V there is a clear reference to the Earl of Essex's campaign in Ireland. Essex set out from London on March 27, 1599 [see note (p. 139) on p. 113 l. 27] accompanied by a vast and cheering mob, which expected him shortly to return in like triumph. The campaign was a miserable failure, and in a few weeks rumours were reaching the City that things were going badly. At this time Shakespeare's Company – the Lord Chamberlain's players as they then were – were playing in the little Curtain playhouse in Shoreditch, waiting for their new playhouse, the Globe on the Bankside, to be completed.

Henry the Fifth was the sequel to the Second Part of *Henry the Fourth*, which ended with the death of Henry the Fourth and the accession of Prince Hal, who had immediately cast off his wild companions, and shown that he was determined to be the ideal King. The two parts of *Henry the Fourth* were produced in the autumn and spring of 1597–8. They were very successful, not only because Prince Hal was a favourite hero, but also because they included the Fat Knight, Sir John Falstaff, who was the most popular of all Shakespeare's characters. Indeed, at the end of the Second Part of *Henry the Fourth* the Epilogue promised that 'if you be not too much cloyed with fat meat, our humble author will continue the story, with Sir John in it, and make you merry with fair Katharine of France.' This promise was not fulfilled. Although the Falstaff gang – Bardolph, Pistol, Mistress Quickly and the boy – reappear, with a newcomer in Corporal Nym, Falstaff himself dies behind the scenes.

Much had happened in the interval of a year which separated *Henry the Fifth* from its predecessor. Ben Jonson's comedy *Every Man in his Humour*, which Shakespeare's company acted in September, 1598, started a new fashion for realism in drama, and in the apologetic tones of the Choruses in *Henry the Fifth*, Shakespeare showed that he was himself self-conscious of the unreality of attempting to portray mighty events with the meagre equipment of the Curtain playhouse.

The story of *Henry the Fifth* was taken from Ralph Holinshed's *Chronicles*, which Shakespeare had already used for his other history plays. Holinshed gave most of the incidents for the serious parts of the play, and at times Shakespeare followed his source closely, taking over even phrases and sentences. The King's speech, for example, to the abashed conspirators in Act II, Scene 2 (pp. 45–7) was recorded in the *Chronicles* thus:

'Having thus *conspired* the death and destruction of me, which am the head of the Realm and Governor of the people, it may be, no doubt, but that you likewise have sworn the confusion of all that are here with me, and also the *desolation* of your own country. To what horror, O Lord, for any true English heart to consider, that such an execrable iniquity should ever so bewrap you, as for pleasing of a foreign enemy to imbrue your hands in your blood, and to ruin your own native soil. *Revenge* herein *touching* my *person*, though I *seek* not; yet for the safeguard of you, my dear friends, and for due preservation of all sorts, I am by office to cause example to be shewed. *Get ye hence therefore, ye poor miserable wretches*, to the receiving of *your* just reward; wherein *God's* majesty *give you* grace of *His mercy and repentance of your* heinous *offences*. And so immediately they were had to execution.' [*Shakespeare's Holinshed*, By W. G. Boswell-Stone, pp. 176–7.]

Apart from Holinshed, there were already plays on Henry the Fifth, who, like other national heroes, had become a legendary figure. Any play had therefore to include some episodes recalling his wild youth, his habit of passing disguised amongst common men, his blunt wooing of the French Princess. They were already available to Shakespeare in the recently published old play, *The Famous Victories of Henry the Fifth*, and in the common talk of playgoers.

Whilst the scenes of serious history follow Holinshed, the comic scenes come nearer home. In the years when Shakespeare was writing his history plays there were continual wars in France, in Spain, and in Ireland. Captains and soldiers, reputable (as Fluellen or Gower) or shady (as Pistol, Bardolph and Nym) were well known in London, hanging about the Court in hope of a new command, or in the taverns remembering 'with advantages' their old battles. In the early weeks of 1599 they were particularly in evidence in London, as they swarmed round Essex House, where Essex was selecting the officers who were to accompany him to Ireland.

The full text of *Henry the Fifth* was first published in the First Folio in 1623; but a pirated version had appeared in 1600, entitled

'THE CRONICLE HISTORY OF HENRY THE FIFT, With his battell fought at *Agin Court in France*. Togither with *Auntient Pistoll. As it had bene sundry times played by the Right honorable the Lord Chamberlaine his seruants.* LONDON. Printed by *Thomas Creede*, for Tho. Millington, and John Busby. And are to be sold at his house in Carter Lane, next the Powle head. 1600.'

This text is incredibly bad, and was either taken down in the playhouse by an incompetent shorthand writer or else put together from memory. It may have been composed for some strolling company, but more probably it was a printer's venture. Shakespeare's plays by 1600 were popular and sure of sale. As a general principle the Company did not allow them to be printed, for there was no copyright in playbooks. Printers, however, could obtain a copyright in their own books by entering them in the Stationers' Register, and at times the Company arranged with a friendly printer to cover the copyright of a popular play by entering it in his own name. This was done with *Henry the Fifth*, which was entered on August 4th, 1600, to James Roberts with the note that it was to be 'stayed'. Apparently Millington and Busby risked prosecution.

The quarto text is very short, omits all the choruses, and many speeches and incidents, and feebly paraphrases the rest. Thus – to take the Quarto at its best – the King's prayer (p. 90, l. 6) is reproduced:

O God of battels steele my souldiers harts,
Take from them now the sence of rekconing.
That the apposed multitudes which stand before them,
May not appall their courage.
O not to day, not to day o God,
Thinke on the fault my father made,
In compassing the crowne.
I *Richards* bodie haue interred new,

And on it hath bestowd more contrite teares,
Then from it issued forced drops of blood:
A hundred men haue I in yearly pay,
Which euery day their withered hands hold vp
To heauen to pardon blood,
And I haue built two chanceries, more wil I do:
Tho all that I can do, is all too litle.

The text in the Folio is fairly well printed. The printer mistook a few words, and was badly puzzled by the passages of dialogue in French. He divided the play into five Acts, but gave no scene divisions, and he made a mistake in the Act divisions. He omitted *Act Two* before the Second Chorus, and then finding that as he came nearer the end there would only be four Acts, he made a new Act division in the middle of the battle of Agincourt, at the end of Act Four, Scene Six.

The Folio text has its own peculiarities. It differs from modern usage in several ways, particularly in spelling, punctuation and use of capitals. The modern custom is to punctuate according to syntax, the Elizabethan to punctuate for reading aloud. Capital letters are used very freely. Place headings, showing the locality of a scene, are not given.

In the present text, the Folio has been followed closely. Spelling is modernized, but the original punctuation and arrangement have been left, except where they seemed obviously wrong; and a few emendations, generally accepted by editors, have been made. The reader who is familiar with the 'accepted text' may thus at first sight find certain unfamiliarities, but the text is nearer to Shakespeare's own version.

The Life of Henry the Fifth

THE ACTORS' NAMES

CHORUS
KING HENRY the Fifth
DUKE OF GLOUCESTER } brothers to the King
DUKE OF BEDFORD }
DUKE OF EXETER, uncle to the King
DUKE OF YORK, cousin to the King
EARL OF SALISBURY, EARL OF WESTMORELAND, EARL OF WARWICK
ARCHBISHOP OF CANTERBURY
BISHOP OF ELY
EARL OF CAMBRIDGE
LORD SCROOP
SIR THOMAS GREY
SIR THOMAS ERPINGHAM } Captains in the King's army
GOWER }
FLUELLEN }
MACMORRIS }
JAMY }
BATES, COURT, WILLIAMS – Soldiers
PISTOL, NYM, BARDOLPH, Boy, A Herald
CHARLES the Sixth, King of France
LEWIS, the Dolphin
DUKE OF BURGUNDY
DUKE OF ORLEANS
DUKE OF BOURBON
The Constables of France
RAMBURES } French Lords
GRANDPRÉ }
Governor of Harfleur
MONTJOY, a French Herald
Ambassadors to the King of England
ISABEL, Queen of France
KATHARINE, daughter to Charles and Isabel
ALICE, a lady attending on her
Hostess of a tavern in Eastcheap, formerly Mistress Quickly, and now married to Pistol.

I

Enter Prologue.

PROLOGUE: O for a Muse of Fire, that would ascend
The brightest Heaven of invention:
A Kingdom for a stage, Princes to act,
And Monarchs to behold the swelling scene.
Then should the warlike Harry, like himself,
Assume the port of Mars, and at his heels
(Leash'd in, like hounds) should Famine, Sword, and Fire
Crouch for employment. But pardon, gentles all,
The flat unraised spirits, that have dar'd,
On this unworthy scaffold, to bring forth
So great an object. Can this cock-pit hold
The vasty fields of France? Or may we cram
Within this wooden O the very casques
That did affright the air at Agincourt?
O pardon: since a crooked figure may
Attest in little place a million,
And let us, ciphers to this great accompt,
On your imaginary forces work.
Suppose within the girdle of these walls
Are now confin'd two mighty Monarchies,
Whose high, upreared, and abutting fronts,
The perilous narrow Ocean parts asunder.
Piece out our imperfections with your thoughts:
Into a thousand parts divide one man,
And make imaginary puissance.
Think when we talk of horses, that you see them,
Printing their proud hoofs i' th' receiving earth:

For 'tis your thoughts that now must deck our Kings,
Carry them here and there: jumping o'er times;
Turning th' accomplishment of many years
Into an hour-glass: for the which supply,
Admit me Chorus to this History;
Who prologue-like, your humble patience pray,
Gently to hear, kindly to judge our play.
Exit.

I. 1

Enter the two Bishops of Canterbury and Ely.

CANTERBURY: My Lord, I'll tell you, that self Bill is urg'd,
Which in th' eleventh year of the last King's reign
Was like, and had indeed against us pass'd,
But that the scambling and unquiet time
Did push it out of farther question.
ELY: But how my Lord shall we resist it now?
CANTERBURY: It must be thought on: if it pass against us,
We lose the better half of our possession:
For all the temporal lands, which men devout
By testament have given to the Church,
Would they strip from us; being valu'd thus,
As much as would maintain, to the King's honour,
Full fifteen Earls, and fifteen hundred Knights,
Six thousand and two hundred good Esquires:
And to relief of lazars, and weak age
Of indigent faint souls, past corporal toil,
A hundred almshouses, right well suppli'd:
And to the coffers of the King beside,
A thousand pounds by th' year Thus runs the Bill.
ELY: This would drink deep.

CANTERBURY: 'Twould drink the cup and all.
ELY: But what prevention?
CANTERBURY: The King is full of grace, and fair regard.
ELY: And a true lover of the holy Church.
CANTERBURY: The courses of his youth promis'd it not.
The breath no sooner left his father's body,
But that his wildness, mortifi'd in him,
Seem'd to die too: yea, at that very moment,
Consideration like an Angel came,
And whipp'd th' offending Adam out of him;
Leaving his body as a Paradise,
T' envelope and contain celestial spirits.
Never was such a sudden scholar made:
Never came reformation in a flood,
With such a heady currance scouring faults:
Nor never Hydra-headed wilfulness
So soon did lose his seat; and all at once;
As in this King.
ELY: We are blessed in the change.
CANTERBURY: Hear him but reason in divinity;
And all-admiring, with an inward wish
You would desire the King were made a Prelate:
Hear him debate of Common-wealth affairs;
You would say, it hath been all in all his study:
List his discourse of war; and you shall hear
A fearful battle render'd you in music.
Turn him to any cause of policy,
The Gordian Knot of it he will unloose,
Familiar as his garter: that when he speaks,
The air, a charter'd libertine, is still,
And the mute wonder lurketh in men's ears,
To steal his sweet and honey'd sentences:
So that the art and practic part of life,

Must be the mistress to this theoric.
Which is a wonder how his Grace should glean it,
Since his addiction was to courses vain,
His companies unletter'd, rude, and shallow,
His hours fill'd up with riots, banquets, sports;
And never noted in him any study,
Any retirement, any sequestration,
From open haunts and popularity.

ELY: The strawberry grows underneath the nettle,
And wholesome berries thrive and ripen best,
Neighbour'd by fruit of baser quality:
And so the Prince obscur'd his contemplation
Under the veil of wildness, which (no doubt)
Grew like the summer grass, fastest by night,
Unseen, yet crescive in his faculty.

CANTERBURY: It must be so; for miracles are ceased:
And therefore we must needs admit the means,
How things are perfected.

ELY: But my good Lord:
How now for mitigation of this Bill,
Urged by the Commons? Doth his Majesty
Incline to it, or no?

CANTERBURY: He seems indifferent:
Or rather swaying more upon our part,
Than cherishing th' exhibiters against us:
For I have made an offer to his Majesty,
Upon our Spiritual Convocation,
And in regard of causes now in hand,
Which I have open'd to his Grace at large,
As touching France, to give a greater sum,
Than ever at one time the Clergy yet
Did to his predecessors part withal.

ELY: How did this offer seem receiv'd, my Lord?

CANTERBURY: With good acceptance of his Majesty:
Save that there was not time enough to hear,
As I perceiv'd his Grace would fain have done,
The severals and unhidden passages
Of his true titles to some certain Dukedoms,
And generally, to the Crown and seat of France,
Deriv'd from Edward, his great-grandfather.
ELY: What was th' impediment that broke this off?
CANTERBURY: The French Ambassador upon that instant
Crav'd audience; and the hour I think is come,
To give him hearing: is it four o'clock?
ELY: It is.
CANTERBURY: Then go we in, to know his embassy:
Which I could with a ready guess declare,
Before the Frenchman speak a word of it.
ELY: I'll wait upon you, and I long to hear it.

Exeunt.

I. 2

Enter King Henry, Humphrey Duke of Gloucester, Bedford, Warwick, Westmoreland and Exeter.

KING HENRY: Where is my gracious Lord of Canterbury?
EXETER: Not here in presence.
KING HENRY: Send for him, good uncle.
WESTMORELAND: Shall we call in th' Ambassador, my Liege?
KING HENRY: Not yet, my cousin: we would be resolv'd,
Before we hear him, of some things of weight,
That task our thoughts, concerning us and France.

Enter the two Bishops.

CANTERBURY: God and his Angels guard your sacred Throne,

And make you long become it.

KING HENRY: Sure we thank you.
My learned Lord, we pray you to proceed,
And justly and religiously unfold,
Why the Law Salique, that they have in France,
Or should or should not bar us in our claim:
And God forbid, my dear and faithful Lord,
That you should fashion, wrest, or bow your reading,
Or nicely charge your understanding soul,
With opening titles miscreate, whose right
Suits not in native colours with the truth:
For God doth know, how many now in health,
Shall drop their blood, in approbation
Of what your reverence shall incite us to.
Therefore take heed how you impawn our person,
How you awake our sleeping sword of war;
We charge you in the Name of God take heed:
For never two such Kingdoms did contend,
Without much fall of blood, whose guiltless drops
Are every one, a woe, a sore complaint,
'Gainst him, whose wrongs give edge unto the swords,
That make such waste in brief mortality.
Under this conjuration, speak my Lord:
For we will hear, note, and believe in heart,
That what you speak, is in your conscience wash'd,
As pure as sin with Baptism.

CANTERBURY: Then hear me gracious Sovereign, and you Peers,
That owe yourselves, your lives, and services,
To this Imperial Throne. There is no bar
To make against your Highness' claim to France,
But this which they produce from Pharamond,
In terram Salicam mulieres ne succedant,

No woman shall succeed in Salique Land:
Which Salique Land, the French unjustly glose
To be the Realm of France, and Pharamond
The founder of this Law, and female bar.
Yet their own authors faithfully affirm,
That the Land Salique is in Germany,
Between the floods of Sala and of Elbe:
Where Charles the Great having subdu'd the Saxons,
There left behind and settled certain French:
Who holding in disdain the German women,
For some dishonest manners of their life,
Establish'd then this Law; to wit, No female
Should be inheritrix in Salique land:
Which Salique (as I said) 'twixt Elbe and Sala,
Is at this day in Germany, call'd Meisen.
Then doth it well appear, the Salique Law
Was not devised for the Realm of France;
Nor did the French possess the Salique Land,
Until four hundred one and twenty years
After defunction of King Pharamond,
Idly suppos'd the founder of this Law,
Who died within the year of our Redemption,
Four hundred twenty-six: and Charles the Great
Subdu'd the Saxons, and did seat the French
Beyond the River Sala, in the year
Eight hundred five. Besides, their writers say,
King Pepin, which deposed Childeric,
Did as heir general, being descended
Of Blithild, which was daughter to King Clothair,
Make claim and title to the Crown of France.
Hugh Capet also, who usurp'd the Crown
Of Charles the Duke of Lorraine, sole heir male
Of the true line and stock of Charles the Great,

To find his title with some shows of truth:
Though in pure truth it was corrupt and naught,
Convey'd himself as th' heir to th' Lady Lingare,
Daughter to Charlemain, who was the son
To Lewis the Emperor, and Lewis the son
Of Charles the Great: also King Lewis the Tenth,
Who was sole heir to the usurper Capet,
Could not keep quiet in his conscience,
Wearing the Crown of France, till satisfied,
That fair Queen Isabel, his grandmother,
Was lineal of the Lady Ermengare,
Daughter to Charles the foresaid Duke of Lorraine:
By the which marriage, the line of Charles the Great
Was re-united to the Crown of France.
So, that as clear as is the summer's sun,
King Pepin's title, and Hugh Capet's claim,
King Lewis his satisfaction, all appear
To hold in right and title of the female:
So do the Kings of France unto this day.
Howbeit, they would hold up this Salique Law,
To bar your Highness claiming from the female,
And rather choose to hide them in a net,
Than amply to imbar their crooked titles,
Usurp'd from you and your progenitors.

KING HENRY: May I with right and conscience make this claim?

CANTERBURY: The sin upon my head, dread Sovereign:
For in the Book of *Numbers* is it writ,
When the man dies, let the inheritance
Descend unto the daughter. Gracious Lord,
Stand for your own, unwind your bloody flag,
Look back into your mighty ancestors:
Go my dread Lord, to your great-grandsire's tomb,

From whom you claim; invoke his warlike spirit,
And your great-uncle's, Edward the Black Prince,
Who on the French ground play'd a tragedy,
Making defeat on the full power of France:
Whiles his most mighty father on a hill
Stood smiling, to behold his lion's whelp
Forage in blood of French nobility.
O noble English, that could entertain
With half their forces, the full pride of France,
And let another half stand laughing by,
All out of work, and cold for action.

ELY: Awake remembrance of these valiant dead,
And with your puissant arm renew their feats;
You are their heir, you sit upon their Throne:
The blood and courage that renowned them,
Runs in your veins: and my thrice-puissant Liege
Is in the very May-morn of his youth,
Ripe for exploits and mighty enterprises.

EXETER: Your brother Kings and Monarchs of the earth
Do all expect, that you should rouse yourself,
As did the former lions of your blood.

WESTMORELAND: They know your Grace hath cause, and means, and might;
So hath your Highness: never King of England
Had nobles richer, and more loyal subjects,
Whose hearts have left their bodies here in England,
And lie pavilion'd in the fields of France.

CANTERBURY: O let their bodies follow my dear Liege
With blood, and sword and fire, to win your right:
In aid whereof, we of the Spirituality
Will raise your Highness such a mighty sum,
As never did the Clergy at one time
Bring in to any of your ancestors.

KING HENRY: We must not only arm t' invade the French,
But lay down our proportions, to defend
Against the Scot, who will make road upon us,
With all advantages.

CANTERBURY: They of those Marches, gracious Sovereign,
Shall be a wall sufficient to defend
Our inland from the pilfering Borderers.

KING HENRY: We do not mean the coursing snatchers only,
But fear the main intendment of the Scot,
Who hath been still a giddy neighbour to us:
For you shall read, that my great-grandfather
Never went with his forces into France,
But that the Scot, on his unfurnish'd Kingdom,
Came pouring like the tide into a breach,
With ample and brim fulness of his force,
Galling the gleaned land with hot assays,
Girding with grievous siege, castles and towns:
That England being empty of defence,
Hath shook and trembled at th' ill neighbourhood.

CANTERBURY: She hath been then more fear'd than harm'd, my Liege:
For hear her but exampl'd by herself,
When all her chivalry hath been in France,
And she a mourning widow of her nobles,
She hath herself not only well defended,
But taken and impounded as a stray,
The King of Scots: whom she did send to France,
To fill King Edward's fame with prisoner Kings,
And make her Chronicle as rich with praise,
As is the ooze and bottom of the sea
With sunken wrack, and sumless treasuries.

ELY: But there's a saying very old and true,
If that you will France win, then with Scotland first begin.
For once the eagle (England) being in prey,
To her unguarded nest, the weasel (Scot)
Comes sneaking, and so sucks her princely eggs,
Playing the mouse in absence of the cat,
To tear and havoc more than she can eat.

EXETER: It follows then, the cat must stay at home,
Yet that is but a crush'd necessity,
Since we have locks to safeguard necessaries,
And pretty traps to catch the petty thieves.
While that the armed hand doth fight abroad,
Th' advised head defends itself at home:
For government, though high, and low, and lower,
Put into parts, doth keep in one consent,
Congreeing in a full and natural close,
Like music.

CANTERBURY: Therefore doth heaven divide
The state of man in divers functions,
Setting endeavour in continual motion:
To which is fixed as an aim or butt,
Obedience: for so work the honey-bees,
Creatures that by a rule in Nature teach
The Act of Order to a peopled kingdom.
They have a King, and officers of sorts,
Where some like magistrates correct at home:
Others, like Merchants venture trade abroad:
Others, like Soldiers, armed in their stings,
Make boot upon the summer's velvet buds:
Which pillage, they with merry march bring home
To the tent-royal of their Emperor:
Who busied in his majesty surveys
The singing masons building roofs of gold,

The civil Citizens kneading up the honey;
The poor mechanic porters, crowding in
Their heavy burthens at his narrow gate:
The sad-eyed Justice with his surly hum,
Delivering o'er to executors pale
The lazy yawning drone: I this infer,
That many things having full reference
To one consent, may work contrariously,
As many arrows loosed several ways
Come to one mark; as many ways meet in one town,
As many fresh streams meet in one salt sea;
As many lines close in the dial's centre:
So may a thousand actions once afoot,
End in one purpose, and be all well borne
Without defeat. Therefore to France, my Liege,
Divide your happy England into four,
Whereof, take you one quarter into France,
And you withal shall make all Gallia shake.
If we with thrice such powers left at home,
Cannot defend our own doors from the dog,
Let us be worried, and our Nation lose
The name of hardiness and policy.

KING HENRY: Call in the messengers sent from the Dolphin.
Now are we well resolv'd, and by God's help
And yours, the noble sinews of our power,
France being ours, we'll bend it to our awe,
Or break it all to pieces. Or there we'll sit,
(Ruling in large and ample empery,
O'er France, and all her almost kingly Dukedoms,)
Or lay these bones in an unworthy urn,
Tombless, with no remembrance over them:
Either our History shall with full mouth

Speak freely of our acts, or else our grave
Like Turkish mute, shall have a tongueless mouth,
Not worshipp'd with a waxen epitaph.

Enter Ambassadors of France.

Now are we well prepar'd to know the pleasure
Of our fair cousin Dolphin: for we hear,
Your greeting is from him, not from the King.

AMBASSADOR: May't please your Majesty to give us leave
Freely to render what we have in charge:
Or shall we sparingly show you far off
The Dolphin's meaning, and our embassy?

KING HENRY: We are no tyrant, but a Christian King,
Unto whose grace our passion is as subject
As are our wretches fetter'd in our prisons,
Therefore with frank and with uncurbed plainness,
Tell us the Dolphin's mind.

AMBASSADOR: Thus then in few;
Your Highness lately sending into France,
Did claim some certain Dukedoms, in the right
Of your great predecessor, King Edward the Third.
In answer of which claim, the Prince our Master
Says, that you savour too much of your youth,
And bids you be advis'd: There's nought in France,
That can be with a nimble galliard won:
You cannot revel into Dukedoms there.
He therefore sends you meeter for your spirit
This tun of treasure; and in lieu of this,
Desires you let the Dukedoms that you claim
Hear no more of you. This the Dolphin speaks.

KING HENRY: What treasure uncle?

EXETER: Tennis balls, my Liege.

KING HENRY: We are glad the Dolphin is so pleasant with us;

His present, and your pains we thank you for:
When we have match'd our rackets to these balls,
We will in France (by God's grace) play a set,
Shall strike his father's Crown into the hazard.
Tell him, he hath made a match with such a wrangler
That all the courts of France will be disturb'd
With chaces. And we understand him well,
How he comes o'er us with our wilder days,
Not measuring what use we made of them.
We never valu'd this poor seat of England,
And therefore living hence, did give ourself
To barbarous license: as 'tis ever common,
That men are merriest, when they are from home.
But tell the Dolphin, I will keep my state,
Be like a King, and show my sail of greatness,
When I do rouse me in my Throne of France.
For that I have laid by my Majesty,
And plodded like a man for working days:
But I will rise there with so full a glory,
That I will dazzle all the eyes of France,
Yea strike the Dolphin blind to look on us,
And tell the pleasant Prince, this mock of his
Hath turn'd his balls to gun-stones, and his soul
Shall stand sore charged, for the wasteful vengeance
That shall fly with them: for many a thousand widows
Shall this his mock, mock out of their dear husbands;
Mock mothers from their sons, mock castles down:
And some are yet ungotten and unborn,
That shall have cause to curse the Dolphin's scorn.
But this lies all within the will of God,
To whom I do appeal, and in whose name
Tell you the Dolphin, I am coming on,
To venge me as I may, and to put forth

My rightful hand in a well-hallow'd cause.
So get you hence in peace: and tell the Dolphin,
His jest will savour but of shallow wit,
When thousands weep more than did laugh at it.
Convey them with safe conduct. Fare you well.

Exeunt Ambassadors.

EXETER: This was a merry message.

KING HENRY: We hope to make the sender blush at it:
Therefore, my Lords, omit no happy hour,
That may give furth'rance to our expedition:
For we have now no thought in us but France,
Save those to God, that run before our business.
Therefore let our proportions for these wars
Be soon collected, and all things thought upon,
That may with reasonable swiftness add
More feathers to our wings: for God before,
We'll chide this Dolphin at his father's door.
Therefore let every man now task his thought,
That this fair action may on foot be brought.

Exeunt.

II

PROLOGUE

Flourish. Enter Chorus.

CHORUS: Now all the youth of England are on fire,
And silken dalliance in the wardrobe lies:
Now thrive the armourers, and Honour's thought
Reigns solely in the breast of every man.
They sell the pasture now, to buy the horse;
Following the Mirror of all Christian Kings,
With winged heels, as English Mercuries.

For now sits Expectation in the air,
And hides a sword, from hilts unto the point,
With crowns imperial, crowns and coronets,
Promis'd to Harry, and his followers.
The French advis'd by good intelligence
Of this most dreadful preparation,
Shake in their fear, and with pale policy
Seek to divert the English purposes.
O England: model to thy inward greatness,
Like little body with a mighty heart:
What mightst thou do, that honour would thee do,
Were all thy children kind and natural:
But see, thy fault France hath in thee found out,
A nest of hollow bosoms, which he fills
With treacherous crowns, and three corrupted men:
One, Richard Earl of Cambridge, and the second
Henry Lord Scroop of Masham, and the third
Sir Thomas Grey Knight of Northumberland,
Have for the gilt of France, (O guilt indeed)
Confirm'd conspiracy with fearful France,
And by their hands, this grace of Kings must die.
If Hell and Treason hold their promises,
Ere he take ship for France; and in Southampton.
Linger your patience on, and we'll digest
Th' abuse of distance; force a play:
The sum is paid, the traitors are agreed,
The King is set from London, and the scene
Is now transported (gentles) to Southampton,
There is the playhouse now, there must you sit.
And thence to France shall we convey you safe,
And bring you back: charming the narrow seas
To give you gentle pass: for if we may,
We'll not offend one stomach with our play.

But till the King come forth, and not till then,
Unto Southampton do we shift our scene.

Exit.

II. I

Enter Corporal Nym, and Lieutenant Bardolph.

BARDOLPH: Well met Corporal Nym.

NYM: Good morrow Lieutenant Bardolph.

BARDOLPH: What, are Ancient Pistol and you friends yet?

NYM: For my part, I care not: I say little: but when time shall serve, there shall be smiles, but that shall be as it may. I dare not fight, but I will wink and hold out mine iron: it is a simple one, but what though? It will toast cheese, and it will endure cold, as another man's sword will: and there's an end.

BARDOLPH: I will bestow a breakfast to make you friends, and we'll be all three sworn brothers to France: let 't be so good Corporal Nym.

NYM: Faith, I will live so long as I may, that's the certain of it: and when I cannot live any longer, I will do as I may: that is my rest, that is the rendezvous of it.

BARDOLPH: It is certain Corporal, that he is married to Nell Quickly, and certainly she did you wrong, for you were troth-plight to her.

NYM: I cannot tell. Things must be as they may: men may sleep, and they may have their throats about them at that time, and some say, knives have edges: it must be as it may, though patience be a tired mare, yet she will plod, there must be conclusions, well, I cannot tell.

Enter Pistol, and Mistress Quickly.

BARDOLPH; Here comes Ancient Pistol and his wife: good Corporal be patient here. How now mine host Pistol?

PISTOL: Base tike, call'st thou me host, now by this hand I swear I scorn the term: nor shall my Nell keep lodgers.

MISTRESS QUICKLY: No by my troth, not long: for we cannot lodge and board a dozen or fourteen gentlewomen that live honestly by the prick of their needles, but it will be thought we keep a bawdy house straight. (*Nym and Pistol draw.*) O welladay Lady, if he be not drawn now, we shall see wilful adultery and murder committed.

BARDOLPH: Good Lieutenant, good Corporal, offer nothing here.

NYM: Pish.

PISTOL: Pish for thee, Iceland dog: thou prickear'd cur of Iceland.

MISTRESS QUICKLY: Good Corporal Nym show thy valour, and put up your sword.

NYM: Will you shog off? I would have you solus.

PISTOL: Solus, egregious dog? O viper vile; the solus in thy most mervailous face, the solus in thy teeth, and in thy throat, and in thy hateful lungs, yea in thy maw perdy; and which is worse, within thy nasty mouth. I do retort the solus in thy bowels, for I can take, and Pistol's cock is up, and flashing fire will follow.

NYM: I am not Barbason, you cannot conjure me: I have an humour to knock you indifferently well: if you grow foul with me Pistol, I will scour you with my rapier, as I may, in fair terms. If you would walk off, I would prick your guts a little in good terms, as I may, and that's the humour of it.

PISTOL: O braggart vile, and damned furious wight,
The grave doth gape, and doting death is near,
Therefore exhale.

BARDOLPH: Hear me, hear me what I say: he that strikes

the first stroke, I'll run him up to the hilts, as I am a soldier.

PISTOL: An oath of mickle might, and fury shall abate. Give me thy fist, thy fore-foot to me give: thy spirits are most tall.

NYM: I will cut thy throat one time or other in fair terms, that is the humour of it.

PISTOL: *Couple a gorge*, that is the word. I thee defy again. O hound of Crete, think'st thou my spouse to get? No, to the spital go, and from the powdering-tub of infamy, fetch forth the lazar kite of Cressid's kind, Doll Tearsheet, she by name, and her espouse. I have, and I will hold the quondam Quickly for the only she: and *pauca*, there's enough to go to.

Enter the Boy.

BOY: Mine host Pistol, you must come to my master, and your hostess: he is very sick, and would to bed. Good Bardolph, put thy face between his sheets, and do the office of a warming-pan: faith, he's very ill.

BARDOLPH: Away you rogue.

MISTRESS QUICKLY: By my troth he'll yield the crow a pudding one of these days: the King has killed his heart. Good husband come home presently.

Exit.

BARDOLPH: Come, shall I make you two friends. We must to France together: why the devil should we keep knives to cut one another's throats?

PISTOL: Let floods o'erswell, and fiends for food howl on.

NYM: You'll pay me the eight shillings I won of you at betting?

PISTOL: Base is the slave that pays.

NYM: That now I will have: that's the humour of it.

PISTOL: As manhood shall compound: push home.

They draw.

BARDOLPH: By this sword, he that makes the first thrust, I'll kill him: by this sword, I will.

PISTOL: Sword is an oath, and oaths must have their course.

BARDOLPH: Corporal Nym, and thou wilt be friends be friends, and thou wilt not, why then be enemies with me too: prithee put up.

PISTOL: A noble shalt thou have, and present pay, and liquor likewise will I give to thee, and friendship shall combine, and brotherhood. I'll live by Nym, and Nym shall live by me, is not this just? For I shall sutler be unto the camp, and profits will accrue. Give me thy hand.

NYM: I shall have my noble?

PISTOL: In cash, most justly paid.

NYM: Well, then that's the humour of 't.

Enter Hostess.

MISTRESS QUICKLY: As ever you came of women, come in quickly to Sir John: Ah, poor heart, he is so shak'd of a burning quotidian tertian, that it is most lamentable to behold. Sweet men, come to him.

NYM: The King hath run bad humours on the Knight, that's the even of it.

PISTOL: Nym, thou hast spoke the right, his heart is fracted and corroborate.

NYM: The King is a good King, but it must be as it may: he passes some humours, and careers.

PISTOL: Let us condole the Knight, for (lambkins) we will live.

II. 2

Enter Exeter, Bedford, and Westmoreland.

BEDFORD: 'Fore God his Grace is bold to trust these traitors.

EXETER: They shall be apprehended by and by.
WESTMORELAND: How smooth and even they do bear themselves,
As if allegiance in their bosoms sat
Crowned with faith, and constant loyalty.
BEDFORD: The King hath note of all that they intend,
By interception, which they dream not of.
EXETER: Nay, but the man that was his bedfellow,
Whom he hath dull'd and cloy'd with gracious favours;
That he should for a foreign purse, so sell
His Sovereign's life to death and treachery.

Sound Trumpets.

Enter King Henry, Scroop, Cambridge, and Grey.

KING HENRY: Now sits the wind fair, and we will aboard.
My Lord of Cambridge, and my kind Lord of Masham,
And you my gentle Knight, give me your thoughts:
Think you not that the powers we bear with us
Will cut their passage through the force of France?
Doing the execution, and the act,
For which we have in head assembled them.
SCROOP: No doubt my Liege, if each man do his best.
KING HENRY: I doubt not that, since we are well persuaded
We carry not a heart with us from hence,
That grows not in a fair consent with ours:
Nor leave not one behind, that doth not wish
Success and conquest to attend on us.
CAMBRIDGE: Never was Monarch better fear'd and lov'd,
Than is your Majesty; there's not I think a subject
That sits in heart-grief and uneasiness
Under the sweet shade of your government.
GREY: True: those that were your father's enemies,
Have steep'd their galls in honey, and do serve you
With hearts create of duty, and of zeal.

KING HENRY: We therefore have great cause of thankfulness,
And shall forget the office of our hand
Sooner than quittance of desert and merit,
According to the weight and worthiness.
SCROOP: So service shall with steeled sinews toil,
And labour shall refresh itself with hope
To do your Grace incessant services.
KING HENRY: We judge no less. Uncle of Exeter,
Enlarge the man committed yesterday,
That rail'd against our person: we consider
It was excess of wine that set him on,
And on his more advice, we pardon him.
SCROOP: That's mercy, but too much security:
Let him be punish'd Sovereign, lest example
Breed (by his sufferance) more of such a kind
KING HENRY: O let us be yet merciful.
CAMBRIDGE: So may your Highness, and yet punish too.
GREY: Sir, you show great mercy if you give him life,
After the taste of much correction.
KING HENRY: Alas, your too much love and care of me,
Are heavy orisons 'gainst this poor wretch:
If little faults proceeding on distemper,
Shall not be wink'd at, how shall we stretch our eye
When capital crimes, chew'd, swallow'd, and digested,
Appear before us? We'll yet enlarge that man,
Though Cambridge, Scroop, and Grey, in their dear care
And tender preservation of our person
Would have him punish'd. And now to our French causes,
Who are the late commissioners?
CAMBRIDGE: I one my Lord,
Your Highness bade me ask for it to-day.
SCROOP: So did you me my Liege.

GREY: And I my royal Sovereign.

KING HENRY: Then Richard Earl of Cambridge, there is yours:
There yours Lord Scroop of Masham, and Sir Knight:
Grey of Northumberland, this same is yours:
Read them, and know I know your worthiness.
My Lord of Westmoreland, and uncle Exeter,
We will aboard to night. Why how now gentlemen?
What see you in those papers, that you lose
So much complexion? Look ye how they change:
Their cheeks are paper. Why, what read you there,
That hath so cowarded and chas'd your blood
Out of appearance?

CAMBRIDGE: I do confess my fault,
And do submit me to your Highness' mercy.

GREY:
SCROOP: } To which we all appeal.

KING HENRY: The mercy that was quick in us but late,
By your own counsel is suppress'd and kill'd:
You must not dare (for shame) to talk of mercy,
For your own reasons turn into your bosoms,
As dogs upon their masters, worrying you:
See you my Princes, and my noble Peers,
These English monsters: my Lord of Cambridge here,
You know how apt our love was, to accord
To furnish him with all appertinents
Belonging to his honour; and this man,
Hath for a few light crowns, lightly conspir'd
And sworn unto the practices of France
To kill us here in Hampton. To the which,
This Knight no less for bounty bound to us
Than Cambridge is, hath likewise sworn. But O,
What shall I say to thee Lord Scroop, thou cruel,

Ingrateful, savage, and inhuman creature?
Thou that didst bear the key of all my counsels,
That knew'st the very bottom of my soul,
That (almost) might'st have coin'd me into gold,
Wouldst thou have practis'd on me, for thy use?
May it be possible, that foreign hire
Could out of thee extract one spark of evil
That might annoy my finger? 'Tis so strange,
That though the truth of it stands off as gross
As black and white, my eye will scarcely see it
Treason and murther, ever kept together,
As two yoke-devils sworn to either's purpose,
Working so grossly in a natural cause,
That admiration did not hoop at them.
But thou ('gainst all proportion) didst bring in
Wonder to wait on treason, and on murther:
And whatsoever cunning fiend it was
That wrought upon thee so preposterously,
Hath got the voice in hell for excellence:
All other devils that suggest by treasons,
Do botch and bungle up damnation,
With patches, colours, and with forms being fetch'd
From glist'ring semblances of piety:
But he that temper'd thee, bade thee stand up,
Gave thee no instance why thou shouldst do treason,
Unless to dub thee with the name of Traitor.
If that same demon that hath gull'd thee thus,
Should with his lion-gait walk the whole world,
He might return to vasty Tartar back,
And tell the legions, I can never win
A soul so easy as that Englishman's.
Oh, how hast thou with jealousy infected
The sweetness of affiance? Show men dutiful,

Why so didst thou: seem they grave and learned?
Why so didst thou. Come they of noble family?
Why so didst thou. Seem they religious?
Why so didst thou. Or are they spare in diet,
Free from gross passion, or of mirth, or anger,
Constant in spirit, not swerving with the blood,
Garnish'd and deck'd in modest complement,
Not working with the eye, without the ear,
And but in purged judgement trusting neither,
Such and so finely bolted didst thou seem:
And thus thy fall hath left a kind of blot,
To mark the full fraught man, and best indued
With some suspicion; I will weep for thee.
For this revolt of thine, methinks is like
Another fall of Man. Their faults are open,
Arrest them to the answer of the Law,
And God acquit them of their practices.

EXETER: I arrest thee of high treason, by the name of Richard Earl of Cambridge.
I arrest thee of high treason, by the name of Henry Lord Scroop of Masham.
I arrest thee of high treason, by the name of Thomas Grey, Knight of Northumberland.

SCROOP: Our purposes, God justly hath discover'd,
And I repent my fault more than my death,
Which I beseech your Highness to forgive,
Although my body pay the price of it.

CAMBRIDGE: For me, the gold of France did not seduce,
Although I did admit it as a motive,
The sooner to effect what I intended:
But God be thanked for prevention,
Which I in sufferance heartily will rejoice,

Beseeching God, and you, to pardon me.

GREY: Never did faithful subject more rejoice
At the discovery of most dangerous treason,
Than I do at this hour joy o'er myself,
Prevented from a damned enterprise;
My fault, but not my body, pardon Sovereign.

KING HENRY: God quit you in his mercy: hear your sentence.
You have conspir'd against our royal person,
Join'd with an enemy proclaim'd, and from his coffers,
Receiv'd the golden earnest of our death;
Wherein you would have sold your King to slaughter,
His Princes, and his Peers to servitude,
His subjects to oppression, and contempt,
And his whole Kingdom into desolation:
Touching our person, seek we no revenge,
But we our Kingdom's safety must so tender,
Whose ruin you have sought, that to her Laws
We do deliver you. Get you therefore hence,
(Poor miserable wretches) to your death:
The taste whereof, God of his mercy give
You patience to endure, and true repentance
Of all your dear offences. Bear them hence.

Exeunt Cambridge, Scroop and Grey guarded.

Now Lords, for France: the enterprise whereof
Shall be to you as us, like glorious.
We doubt not of a fair and lucky war,
Since God so graciously hath brought to light
This dangerous treason, lurking in our way,
To hinder our beginnings. We doubt not now,
But every rub is smoothed on our way.
Then forth, dear countrymen: let us deliver
Our puissance into the hand of God,

Putting it straight in expedition.
Cheerly to sea, the signs of War advance,
No King of England, if not King of France.
Flourish. Exeunt.

II. 3

Enter Pistol, Nym, Bardolph, Boy and Hostess.

MISTRESS QUICKLY: Prithee honey sweet husband, let me bring thee to Staines.

PISTOL: No: for my manly heart doth earn. Bardolph, be blithe: Nym, rouse thy vaunting veins: Boy, bristle thy courage up: for Falstaff he is dead, and we must earn therefore.

BARDOLPH: Would I were with him, wheresome'er he is, either in Heaven, or in Hell.

MISTRESS QUICKLY: Nay sure, he's not in Hell: he's in Arthur's bosom, if ever man went to Arthur's bosom: a' made a finer end, and went away and it had been any christom child: a' parted ev'n just between twelve and one, ev'n at the turning o' th' tide: for after I saw him fumble with the sheets, and play with flowers, and smile upon his fingers' end, I knew there was but one way: for his nose was as sharp as a pen, and a' talk of green fields. How now, Sir John? (quoth I) what man? be o' good cheer. So a' cried out, God, God, God, three or four times: now I, to comfort him, bid him a' should not think of God; I hop'd there was no need to trouble himself with any such thoughts yet: so a' bad me lay more clothes on his feet: I put my hand into the bed, and felt them, and they were as cold as any stone: then I felt to his knees, and so uppear'd, and upward, and all was as cold as any stone.

NYM: They say he cried out of sack.

MISTRESS QUICKLY: Ay, that a' did.

BARDOLPH: And of women.

MISTRESS QUICKLY: Nay, that a' did not.

BOY: Yes that a' did, and said they were devils incarnate.

MISTRESS QUICKLY: A' could never abide carnation, 'twas a colour he never lik'd.

BOY: A' said once, the Devil would have him about women.

MISTRESS QUICKLY: A' did in some sort (indeed) handle women: but then he was rheumatic, and talked of the Whore of Babylon.

BOY: Do you not remember a' saw a flea stick upon Bardolph's nose, and a' said it was a black soul burning in Hell?

BARDOLPH: Well, the fuel is gone that maintain'd that fire: that's all the riches I got in his service.

NYM: Shall we shog? the King will be gone from Southampton.

PISTOL: Come, let's away. My love, give me thy lips: look to my chattels, and my movables: let senses rule: the word is, Pitch and pay: trust none: for oaths are straws, men's faiths are wafer-cakes, and hold-fast is the only dog: my duck, therefore *caveto* be thy councillor. Go, clear thy crystals. Yoke-fellows in arms, let us to France, like horse-leeches my boys, to suck, to suck, the very blood to suck.

BOY: And that's but unwholesome food, they say.

PISTOL: Touch her soft mouth, and march.

BARDOLPH: Farewell hostess.

NYM: I cannot kiss, that is the humour of it: but adieu.

PISTOL: Let huswifery appear: keep close, I thee command.

MISTRESS QUICKLY: Farewell: adieu.

Exeunt.

II.4

Flourish. Enter the French King, the Dolphin, the Dukes of Berri and Bretagne, the Constable, and others.

FRENCH KING: Thus comes the English with full power upon us,
And more than carefully it us concerns,
To answer royally in our defences.
Therefore the Dukes of Berri and of Bretagne,
Of Brabant and of Orleans, shall make forth,
And you Prince Dolphin, with all swift dispatch
To line and new repair our towns of war
With men of courage, and with means defendant:
For England his approaches makes as fierce,
As waters to the sucking of a gulf.
It fits us then to be as provident,
As fear may teach us, out of late examples
Left by the fatal and neglected English,
Upon our fields.

DOLPHIN: My most redoubted father,
It is most meet we arm us 'gainst the foe:
For peace itself should not so dull a Kingdom,
(Though war nor no known quarrel were in question)
But that defences, musters, preparations,
Should be maintain'd, assembled, and collected,
As were a war in expectation.
Therefore I say, 'tis meet we all go forth,
To view the sick and feeble parts of France:
And let us do it with no show of fear,
No, with no more, than if we heard that England
Were busied with a Whitsun morris-dance:
For, my good Liege, she is so idly king'd,

Her sceptre so fantastically borne,
By a vain, giddy, shallow humorous youth,
That fear attends her not.

CONSTABLE: O peace, Prince Dolphin,
You are too much mistaken in this King:
Question your Grace the late ambassadors,
With what great state he heard their embassy,
How well supplied with noble Councillors,
How modest in exception; and withal,
How terrible in constant resolution:
And you shall find his vanities forespent,
Were but the outside of the Roman Brutus,
Covering discretion with a coat of folly;
As gardeners do with ordure hide those roots
That shall first spring, and be most delicate.

DOLPHIN: Well, 'tis not so, my Lord High Constable.
But though we think it so, it is no matter:
In cases of defence, 'tis best to weigh
The enemy more mighty than he seems,
So the proportions of defence are fill'd:
Which of a weak and niggardly projection,
Doth like a miser spoil his coat, with scanting
A little cloth.

FRENCH KING: Think we King Harry strong:
And Princes, look you strongly arm to meet him.
The kindred of him hath been flesh'd upon us:
And he is bred out of that bloody strain,
That haunted us in our familiar paths:
Witness our too much memorable shame,
When Cressy battle fatally was struck,
And all our Princes captiv'd, by the hand
Of that black name, Edward, Black Prince of Wales:
Whiles that his mountain sire, on mountain standing

Up in the air, crown'd with the golden sun,
Saw his heroical seed, and smil'd to see him
Mangle the work of Nature, and deface
The patterns, that by God and by French fathers
Had twenty years been made. This is a stem
Of that victorious stock: and let us fear
The native mightiness and fate of him.

Enter a Messenger.

MESSENGER: Ambassadors from Harry King of England,
Do crave admittance to your Majesty.

FRENCH KING: We'll give them present audience.
Go, and bring them.
You see this chase is hotly follow'd, fri:nds.

DOLPHIN: Turn head, and stop pursuit: for coward dogs
Most spend their mouths, when what they seem to threaten
Runs far before them. Good my Sovereign
Take up the English short, and let them know
Of what a monarchy you are the head:
Self-love, my Liege, is not so vile a sin,
As self-neglecting.

Enter Exeter.

FRENCH KING: From our Brother of England?

EXETER: From him, and thus he greets your Majesty:
He wills you in the name of God Almighty,
That you divest yourself, and lay apart
The borrow'd glories, that by gift of Heaven,
By Law of Nature, and of Nations, 'longs
To him and to his heirs, namely the Crown,
And all wide-stretched honours, that pertain
By custom, and the ordinance of times,
Unto the Crown of France: that you may know
'Tis no sinister, nor no awkward claim,

Pick'd from the worm-holes of long-vanish'd days,
Nor from the dust of old oblivion rak'd,
He sends you this most memorable line,
In every branch truly demonstrative;
Willing you overlook this pedigree:
And when you find him evenly deriv'd
From his most fam'd, of famous ancestors,
Edward the Third; he bids you then resign
Your Crown and Kingdom, indirectly held
From him, the native and true challenger.

FRENCH KING: Or else what follows?

EXETER: Bloody constraint: for if you hide the Crown
Even in your hearts, there will he rake for it.
Therefore in fierce tempest is he coming,
In thunder and in earthquake, like a Jove:
That if requiring fail, he will compel.
And bids you, in the bowels of the Lord,
Deliver up the Crown, and to take mercy
On the poor souls, for whom this hungry War
Opens his vasty jaws; and on your head
Turning the widows' tears, the orphans' cries,
The dead men's blood, the pining maiden's groans,
For husbands, fathers and betrothed lovers,
That shall be swallow'd in this controversy.
This is his claim, his threatening, and my message:
Unless the Dolphin be in presence here;
To whom expressly I bring greeting too.

FRENCH KING: For us, we will consider of this further:
To-morrow shall you bear our full intent
Back to our Brother of England.

DOLPHIN: For the Dolphin,
I stand here for him: what to him from England?

EXETER: Scorn and defiance, slight regard, contempt,

And any thing that may not misbecome
The mighty sender, doth he prize you at.
Thus says my King: and if your father's Highness
Do not, in grant of all demands at large,
Sweeten the bitter mock you sent his Majesty;
He'll call you to so hot an answer of it,
That caves and womby vaultages of France
Shall chide your trespass, and return your mock
In second accent of his ordinance.

DOLPHIN: Say: if my father render fair return,
It is against my will: for I desire
Nothing but odds with England.
To that end, as matching to his youth and vanity,
I did present him with the Paris balls.

EXETER: He'll make your Paris Louvre shake for it,
Were it the mistress-court of mighty Europe:
And be assur'd, you'll find a difference,
As we his subjects have in wonder found,
Between the promise of his greener days,
And these he masters now: now he weighs time
Even to the utmost grain: that you shall read
In your own losses, if he stay in France.

FRENCH KING: To-morrow shall you know our mind at full.

Flourish.

EXETER: Dispatch us with all speed, lest that our King
Come here himself to question our delay;
For he is footed in this land already.

FRENCH KING: You shall be soon dispatch'd, with fair conditions.
A night is but small breath, and little pause,
To answer matters of this consequence.

Exeunt.

III

Flourish. Enter Chorus.

CHORUS: Thus with imagin'd wing our swift scene flies,
In motion of no less celerity than that of thought.
Suppose, that you have seen
The well-appointed King at Hampton pier,
Embark his royalty: and his brave fleet,
With silken streamers, the young Phœbus fanning;
Play with your fancies: and in them behold,
Upon the hempen tackle, ship-boys climbing;
Hear the shrill whistle, which doth order give
To sounds confus'd: behold the threaden sails,
Borne with th' invisible and creeping wind,
Draw the huge bottoms through the furrowed sea,
Breasting the lofty surge. O, do but think
You stand upon the rivage, and behold
A city on th' inconstant billows dancing:
For so appears this fleet majestical,
Holding due course to Harfleur. Follow, follow:
Grapple your minds to sternage of this navy,
And leave your England as dead midnight, still,
Guarded with grandsires, babies, and old women,
Either past, or not arriv'd to pith and puissance:
For who is he, whose chin is but enrich'd
With one appearing hair, that will not follow
These cull'd and choice-drawn cavaliers to France?
Work, work your thoughts, and therein see a siege:
Behold the ordinance on their carriages,
With fatal mouths gaping on girded Harfleur.
Suppose th' Ambassador from the French comes back:
Tells Harry, that the King doth offer him

Katharine his daughter, and with her to dowry,
Some petty and unprofitable Dukedoms.
The offer likes not: and the nimble gunner
With linstock now the devilish cannon touches,

Alarum, and chambers go off.

And down goes all before them. Still be kind,
And eke out our performance with your mind.

Exit.

III. I

Enter the King, Exeter, Bedford and Gloucester. Alarum: Scaling ladders at Harfleur.

KING HENRY: Once more unto the breach,
Dear friends, once more;
Or close the wall up with our English dead:
In peace, there's nothing so becomes a man,
As modest stillness, and humility:
But when the blast of war blows in our ears,
Then imitate the action of the tiger:
Stiffen the sinews, summon up the blood,
Disguise fair Nature with hard-favour'd rage:
Then lend the eye a terrible aspect:
Let it pry through the portage of the head,
Like the brass cannon: let the brow o'erwhelm it,
As fearfully, as doth a galled rock
O'erhang and jutty his confounded base,
Swill'd with the wild and wasteful ocean.
Now set the teeth, and stretch the nostril wide,
Hold hard the breath, and bend up every spirit
To his full height. On, on, you noblest English,
Whose blood is fet from fathers of war-proof:
Fathers, that like so many Alexanders,

Have in these parts from morn till even fought,
And sheath'd their swords, for lack of argument.
Dishonour not your mothers: now attest,
That those whom you call'd fathers, did beget you.
Be copy now to men of grosser blood,
And teach them how to war. And you good yeomen,
Whose limbs were made in England; show us here
The mettle of your pasture: let us swear,
That you are worth your breeding: which I doubt not:
For there is none of you so mean and base,
That hath not noble lustre in your eyes.
I see you stand like greyhounds in the slips,
Straining upon the start. The game's afoot:
Follow your spirit; and upon this charge,
Cry, God for Harry, England, and Saint George.

Exeunt. Alarum, and chambers go off.

III.2

Enter Nym, Bardolph, Pistol and Boy.

BARDOLPH: On, on, on, on, on, to the breach, to the breach.

NYM: Pray thee Corporal stay, the knocks are too hot: and for mine own part, I have not a case of lives: the humour of it is too hot, that is the very plain-song of it.

PISTOL: The plain-song is most just: for humours do abound: knocks go and come: God's vassals drop and die: and sword and shield, in bloody field, doth win immortal fame.

BOY: Would I were in an alehouse in London, I would give all my fame for a pot of ale, and safety.

PISTOL: And I: if wishes would prevail with me, my purpose should not fail with me; but thither would I hie.

BOY: As duly, but not as truly, as bird doth sing on bough.

Enter Fluellen.

FLUELLEN: Up to the breach, you dogs; avaunt you cullions.

PISTOL: Be merciful great Duke to men of mould: abate thy rage, abate thy manly rage; abate thy rage, great Duke. Good bawcock bate thy rage: use lenity sweet chuck.

NYM: These be good humours: your honour wins bad humours.

Exit Nym and Pistol.

BOY: As young as I am, I have observ'd these three swashers: I am boy to them all three, but all they three, though they would serve me, could not be man to me; for indeed three such antics do not amount to a man: for Bardolph, he is white-liver'd, and red-fac'd; by the means whereof, a' faces it out, but fights not: for Pistol, he hath a killing tongue, and a quiet sword; by the means whereof, a' breaks words, and keeps whole weapons: for Nym, he hath heard, that men of few words are the best men, and therefore he scorns to say his prayers, lest a' should be thought a coward: but his few bad words are match'd with as few good deeds; for a' never broke any man's head but his own, and that was against a post, when he was drunk. They will steal any thing, and call it purchase. Bardolph stole a lute-case, bore it twelve leagues, and sold it for three half-pence. Nym and Bardolph are sworn brothers in filching: and in Callice they stole a fire-shovel. I knew by that piece of service, the men would carry coals. They would have me as familiar with men's pockets, as their gloves or their handkerchers: which makes much against my manhood, if I should take from another's pocket, to put into mine; for it is plain pocketing up of wrongs. I must leave them, and seek some better service: their villainy goes against my weak stomach, and therefore I must cast it up.

Exit.

Enter Gower.

GOWER: Captain Fleullen, you must come presently to the mines; the Duke of Gloucester would speak with you.

FLUELLEN: To the mines? Tell you the Duke, it is not so good to come to the mines: for look you, the mines is not according to the disciplines of the war; the concavities of it is not sufficient: for look you, th' athversary, you may discuss unto the Duke, look you, is digt himself four yard under the counter-mines: by Cheshu, I think a' will plow up all, if there is not better directions.

GOWER: The Duke of Gloucester, to whom the order of the siege is given, is altogether directed by an Irishman, a very valiant gentleman i' faith.

FLUELLEN: It is Captain Macmorris, is it not?

GOWER: I think it be.

FLUELLEN: By Cheshu he is an ass, as in the World, I will verify as much in his beard: he has no more directions in the true disciplines of the wars, look you, of the Roman disciplines, than is a puppy-dog.

Enter Macmorris, and Captain Jamy.

GOWER: Here a' comes, and the Scots captain, Captain Jamy, with him.

FLUELLEN: Captain Jamy is a marvellous falorous gentleman, that is certain, and of great expedition and knowledge in th' aunchient wars, upon my particular knowledge of his directions: by Cheshu he will maintain his argument as well as any military man in the World, in the disciplines of the pristine wars of the Romans.

JAMY: I say gud-day, Captain Fluellen.

FLUELLEN: Godden to your worship, good Captain James.

GOWER: How now Captain Macmorris, have you quit the mines? have the pioners given o'er?

MACMORRIS: By Chrish Law tish ill done: the work ish give over, the trompet sound the retreat. By my hand I swear, and my father's soul, the work ish ill done: it ish give over: I would have blowed up the town, so Chrish save me law in an hour. O tish ill done, tish ill done: by my hand tish ill done.

FLUELLEN: Captain Macmorris, I beseech you now, will you voutsafe me, look you, a few disputations with you, as partly touching or concerning the disciplines of the war, the Roman wars, in the way of argument, look you, and friendly communication: partly to satisfy my opinion, and partly for the satisfaction, look you, of my mind: as touching the direction of the military discipline, that is the point.

JAMY: It sall be vary gud, gud feith, gud Captains bath, and I sall quit you with gud leve, as I may pick occasion: that sall I marry.

MACMORRIS: It is no time to discourse, so Chrish save me: the day is hot, and the weather, and the wars, and the King, and the Dukes: it is no time to discourse; the town is beseeched: and the trumpet call us to the breach, and we talk, and be Chrish do nothing, 'tis shame for us all: so God sa' me 'tis shame to stand still, it is shame by my hand: and there is throats to be cut, and works to be done, and there ish nothing done, so Chrish sa' me law.

JAMY: By the Mess, ere theise eyes of mine take themselves to slomber, ay'll de gud service, or ay'll lig i' th' grund for it: ay, or go to death: and I'll pay 't as valorously as I may, that sall I suerly do, that is the breff and the long: marry, I wad full fain hear some question 'tween you tway.

FLUELLEN: Captain Macmorris, I think, look you, under your correction, there is not many of your nation.

MACMORRIS: Of my Nation? What ish my Nation? Ish a villain, and a bastard, and a knave, and a rascal. What ish my Nation? Who talks of my Nation?

FLUELLEN: Look you, if you take the matter otherwise than is meant, Captain Macmorris, peradventure I shall think you do not use me with that affability, as in discretion you ought to use me, look you, being as good a man as yourself, both in the disciplines of war, and in the derivation of my birth, and in other particularities.

MACMORRIS: I do not know you so good a man as myself: so Chrish save me, I will cut off your head.

GOWER: Gentlemen both, you will mistake each other.

JAMY: A, that's a foul fault.

A parley.

GOWER: The town sounds a parley.

FLUELLEN: Captain Macmorris, when there is more better opportunity to be required, look you, I will be so bold as to tell you, I know the disciplines of war: and there is an end.

Exeunt.

III. 3

Enter the King and all his train before the gates.

KING HENRY: How yet resolves the Governor of the town?
This is the latest parle we will admit:
Therefore to our best mercy give yourselves,
Or like to men proud of destruction,
Defy us to our worst: for as I am a soldier,

A name that in my thoughts becomes me best;
If I begin the battery once again,
I will not leave the half-achieved Harfleur,
Till in her ashes she lie buried.
The gates of Mercy shall be all shut up,
And the flesh'd soldier, rough and hard of heart,
In liberty of bloody hand, shall range
With conscience wide as Hell, mowing like grass
Your fresh fair virgins, and your flow'ring infants.
What is it then to me, if impious War,
Array'd in flames like to the Prince of Fiends,
Do with his smirch'd complexion all fell feats,
Enlink'd to waste and desolation?
What is't to me, when you yourselves are cause,
If your pure maidens fall into the hand
Of hot and forcing violation?
What rein can hold licentious wickedness,
When down the hill he holds his fierce career?
We may as bootless spend our vain command
Upon th' enraged soldiers in their spoil,
As send precepts to the leviathan, to come ashore.
Therefore, you men of Harfleur,
Take pity of your town and of your people,
Whiles yet my soldiers are in my command,
Whiles yet the cool and temperate wind of Grace
O'erblows the filthy and contagious clouds
Of heady murther, spoil, and villainy.
If not: why in a moment look to see
The blind and bloody soldier, with foul hand
Defile the locks of your shrill-shrieking daughters:
Your fathers taken by the silver beards,
And their most reverend heads dash'd to the walls:
Your naked infants spitted upon pikes,

Whiles the mad mothers, with their howls confus'd,
Do break the clouds; as did the wives of Jewry,
At Herod's bloody-hunting slaughtermen.
What say you? will you yield, and this avoid?
Or guilty in defence, be thus destroy'd.

Enter Governor.

GOVERNOR: Our expectation hath this day an end:
The Dolphin, whom of succours we entreated,
Returns us, that his powers are yet not ready,
To raise so great a siege. Therefore great King,
We yield our town and lives to thy soft mercy:
Enter our gates, dispose of us and ours,
For we no longer are defensible.

KING HENRY: Open your gates. Come uncle Exeter,
Go you and enter Harfleur; there remain,
And fortify it strongly 'gainst the French:
Use mercy to them all for us, dear uncle.
The winter coming on, and sickness growing
Upon our soldiers, we will retire to Callice.
To-night in Harfleur will we be your guest,
To-morrow for the march are we addrest.

Flourish, and enter the town.

III. 4

Enter Katharine and Alice, an old gentlewoman.

KATHARINE: *Alice, tu as esté en Angleterre, et tu bien parles le language.*

ALICE: *Un peu Madame.*

KATHARINE: *Je te prie, m'enseignez; il faut que j'apprenne à parler. Comment appellez vous la main en Anglois?*

ALICE: *La main? elle est appellée de hand.*

KATHARINE: *De hand. Et les doigts?*

ALICE: *Les doigts? ma foy, j'oublie les doigts; mais je me souviendray. Les doigts? je pense qu'ils sont appellés de fingres; ouy, de fingres.*

KATHARINE: *La main, de hand; les doigts, de fingres. Je pense que je suis le bon escolier; j'ai gagné deux mots d'Anglois vistement. Comment appellez vous les ongles?*

ALICE: *Les ongles? nous les appellons de nails.*

KATHARINE: *De nails. Escoutez; dites moy, si je parley bien: de hand, de fingres, et de nails.*

ALICE: *C'est bien dict, Madame; il est fort bon Anglois.*

KATHARINE: *Dites moy l'Anglois pour le bras.*

ALICE: *De arme, Madame.*

KATHARINE: *Et le coude?*

ALICE: *D'elbow.*

KATHARINE: *D'elbow. Je me'n fais la répétition de tous les mots que vous m'avez appris dès à présent.*

ALICE: *Il est trop difficile, Madame, comme je pense.*

KATHARINE: *Excusez moy, Alice; escoutez: d'hand, de fingre, de nails, d'arme, de bilbow.*

ALICE: *D'elbow, Madame.*

KATHARINE: *O Seigneur Dieu, je m'en oublie; de elbow. Comment appellez vous le col?*

ALICE: *De nick, Madame.*

KATHARINE: *De nick. Et le menton?*

ALICE: *De chin.*

KATHARINE: *De sin. Le col, de nick; le menton, de sin.*

ALICE: *Ouy. Sauf vostre honneur, en vérite, vous prononcez les môts aussi droict que les natifs d'Angleterre.*

KATHARINE: *Je ne doute point d'apprendre, par la grace de Dieu, et en peu de temps.*

ALICE: *N'avez vous déjà oublié ce que je vous ai enseigné?*

KATHARINE: *Non, je reciterai à vous promptement: d'hand, de fingre, de mailes, –*

ALICE: *De nails, Madame.*

KATHARINE: *De nails, de arm, de ilbow.*

ALICE: *Sauf votre honneur, d'elbow.*

KATHARINE *Ainsi dis-je; d'elbow, de nick, et de sin. Comment appellez-vous le pied et la robe?*

ALICE: *Le foot, Madame; et le coun.*

KATHARINE: *Le foot et le coun; O Seigneur Dieu, ils sont mots de son mauvais, corruptible, gros, et impudique, et non pour les Dames d'honneur d'user: je ne voudrais prononcer ces mots devant les Seigneurs de France pour tout le monde. Foh, le foot et le coun néant-moins. Je réciteray une autre fois ma leçon ensemble: d'hand, de fingre, de nails, d'arm, d'elbow, de nick, de sin, de foot, le coun.*

ALICE: *Excellent, Madame.*

KATHARINE: *C'est assez pour une fois: allons nous à dîner.*

Exeunt.

III. 5

Enter the King of France, the Dolphin, the Duke of Bourbon, the Constable of France and others.

FRENCH KING: 'Tis certain he hath pass'd the river Somme.

CONSTABLE: And if he be not fought withal, my Lord,
Let us not live in France: let us quit all,
And give our vineyards to a barbarous people.

DOLPHIN: O *Dieu vivant:* shall a few sprays of us,
The emptying of our fathers' luxury,
Our scions, put in wild and savage stock,
Spirt up so suddenly into the clouds,
And overlook their grafters?

BOURBON: Normans, but bastard Normans, Norman bastards:

Mort de ma vie, if they march along
Unfought withal, but I will sell my Dukedom,
To buy a slobbery and a dirty farm
In that nook-shotten Isle of Albion.

CONSTABLE: *Dieu de batailles,* where have they this mettle?
Is not their climate foggy, raw, and dull?
On whom, as in despite, the sun looks pale,
Killing their fruit with frowns. Can sodden water,
A drench for sur-rein'd jades, their barley broth,
Decoct their cold blood to such valiant heat?
And shall our quick blood, spirited with wine,
Seem frosty? O, for honour of our land,
Let us not hang like roping icicles
Upon our houses' thatch, whiles a more frosty people
Sweat drops of gallant youth in our rich fields:
Poor we may call them, in their native Lords.

DOLPHIN: By faith and honour,
Our madames mock at us, and plainly say,
Our mettle is bred out, and they will give
Their bodies to the lust of English youth,
To new-store France with bastard warriors.

BOURBON: They bid us to the English dancing-schools,
And teach lavoltas high, and swift corantos,
Saying, our grace is only in our heels,
And that we are most lofty runaways.

FRENCH KING: Where is Montjoy the Herald? speed him hence,
Let him greet England with our sharp defiance.
Up Princes, and with spirit of honour edged,
More sharper than your swords, hie to the field:
Charles Delabreth, High Constable of France,
You Dukes of Orleans, Bourbon, and of Berri,

Alanson, Brabant, Bar, and Burgundy,
Jaques Chatillon, Rambures, Vaudemont,
Beaumont, Grandpré, Roussi, and Falconbridge,
Foix, Lestrale, Bouciqualt, and Charolois,
High Dukes, great Princes, Barons, Lords, and Knights;
For your great seats, now quit you of great shames:
Bar Harry England, that sweeps through our land
With pennons painted in the blood of Harfleur:
Rush on his host, as doth the melted snow
Upon the valleys, whose low vassal seat,
The Alps doth spit, and void his rheum upon.
Go down upon him, you have power enough,
And in a captive chariot, into Roan
Bring him our prisoner.

CONSTABLE: This becomes the great.
Sorry am I his numbers are so few,
His soldiers sick, and famish'd in their march:
For I am sure, when he shall see our army,
He'll drop his heart into the sink of fear,
And for achievement, offer us his ransom.

FRENCH KING: Therefore Lord Constable, haste on Montjoy,
And let him say to England, that we send,
To know what willing ransom he will give.
Prince Dolphin, you shall stay with us in Roan.

DOLPHIN: Not so, I do beseech your Majesty.

FRENCH KING: Be patient, for you shall remain with us.
Now forth Lord Constable, and Princes all,
And quickly bring us word of England's fall.

Exeunt.

III. 6

Enter Captains, English and Welsh, Gower and Fluellen.

GOWER: How now Captain Fluellen, come you from the bridge?

FLUELLEN: I assure you, there is very excellent services committed at the bridge.

GOWER: Is the Duke of Exeter safe?

FLUELLEN: The Duke of Exeter is as magnanimous as Agamemnon, and a man that I love and honour with my soul, and my heart, and my duty, and my life, and my living, and my uttermost power. He is not, God be praised and blessed, any hurt in the world, but keeps the bridge most valiantly, with excellent discipline. There is an aunchient Lieutenant there at the pridge, I think in my very conscience he is as valiant a man as Mark Antony, and he is a man of no estimation in the World, but I did see him do as gallant service.

GOWER: What do you call him?

FLUELLEN: He is call'd Aunchient Pistol.

GOWER: I know him not.

Enter Pistol.

FLUELLEN: Here is the man.

PISTOL: Captain, I beseech thee to do me favours: the Duke of Exeter doth love thee well.

FLUELLEN: Ay, I praise God, and I have merited some love at his hands.

PISTOL: Bardolph, a soldier firm and sound of heart, and of buxom valour, hath by cruel Fate, and giddy Fortune's furious fickle wheel, that goddess blind, that stands upon the rolling restless stone.

FLUELLEN: By your patience, Aunchient Pistol: Fortune

is painted blind, with a muffler afore her eyes, to signify to you, that Fortune is blind; and she is painted also with a wheel, to signify to you, which is the moral of it, that she is turning and inconstant, and mutability, and variation: and her foot, look you, is fixed upon a spherical stone, which rolls, and rolls, and rolls: in good truth, the poet makes a most excellent description of it: Fortune is an excellent moral.

PISTOL: Fortune is Bardolph's foe, and frowns on him: for he hath stolen a pax, and hanged must a' be: a damned death: let gallows gape for dog, let man go free, and let not hemp his wind-pipe suffocate: but Exeter hath given the doom of death, for pax of little price. Therefore go speak, the Duke will hear thy voice: and let not Bardolph's vital thread be cut with edge of penny cord, and vile reproach. Speak Captain for his life, and I will thee requite.

FLUELLEN: Aunchient Pistol, I do partly understand your meaning.

PISTOL: Why then rejoice therefore.

FLUELLEN: Certainly Aunchient, it is not a thing to rejoice at: for if, look you, he were my brother, I would desire the Duke to use his good pleasure, and put him to execution; for discipline ought to be used.

PISTOL: Die, and be damn'd, and *figo* for thy friendship.

FLUELLEN: It is well.

PISTOL: The fig of Spain.

Exit.

FLUELLEN: Very good.

GOWER: Why, this is an arrant counterfeit rascal, I remember him now: a bawd, a cut-purse.

FLUELLEN: I'll assure you, a' uttered as prave words at the pridge, as you shall see in a summer's day: but it is very well: what he has spoke to me, that is well I warrant you, when time is serve.

GOWER: Why 'tis a gull, a fool, a rogue, that now and then goes to the wars, to grace himself at his return into London, under the form of a soldier: and such fellows are perfect in the great Commanders' names and they will learn you by rote where services were done; at such and such a sconce, at such a breach, at such a convoy: who came off bravely, who was shot, who disgrac'd, what terms the enemy stood on: and this they con perfectly in the phrase of war; which they trick up with new-tuned oaths: and what a beard of the General's cut, and a horrid suit of the camp, will do among foaming bottles, and ale-wash'd wits, is wonderful to be thought on: but you must learn to know such slanders of the age, or else you may be marvellously mistook.

FLUELLEN: I tell you what, Captain Gower: I do perceive he is not the man that he would gladly make show to the World he is: if I find a hole in his coat, I will tell him my mind: hark you, the King is coming, and I must speak with him from the pridge.

Drums and colours. Enter the King, Gloucester, and his poor Soldiers.

God pless your Majesty.

KING HENRY: How now Fluellen, camest thou from the bridge?

FLUELLEN: Ay, so please your Majesty: the Duke of Exeter has very gallantly maintain'd the pridge; the French is gone off, look you, and there is gallant and most prave passages: marry, th' athversary was have possession of the pridge, but he is enforced to retire, and the Duke of Exeter is master of the pridge: I can tell your Majesty, the Duke is a prave man.

KING HENRY: What men have you lost, Fluellen?

FLUELLEN: The perdition of th' athversary hath been very great, reasonable great: marry for my part, I think the Duke hath lost never a man, but one that is like to be executed for robbing a church, one Bardolph, if your Majesty know the man: his face is all bubukles and whelks, and knobs, and flames a' fire, and his lips blows at his nose, and it is like a coal of fire, sometimes plue, and sometimes red, but his nose is executed, and his fire's out.

KING HENRY: We would have all such offenders so cut off: and we give express charge, that in our marches through the country, there be nothing compell'd from the villages; nothing taken, but paid for: none of the French upbraided or abused in disdainful language; for when Lenity and Cruelty play for a Kingdom, the gentler gamester is the soonest winner.

Tucket. Enter Montjoy.

MONTJOY: You know me by my habit.

KING HENRY: Well then, I know thee: what shall I know of thee?

MONTJOY: My master's mind.

KING HENRY: Unfold it.

MONTJOY: Thus says my King: Say thou to Harry of England, Though we seem'd dead, we did but sleep: advantage is a better soldier than rashness. Tell him, we could have rebuk'd him at Harfleur, but that we thought not good to bruise an injury, till it were full ripe. Now we speak upon our cue, and our voice is imperial: England shall repent his folly, see his weakness, and admire our sufferance. Bid him therefore consider of his ransom, which must proportion the losses we have borne, the subjects we have lost, the disgrace we have digested;

which in weight to re-answer, his pettiness would bow under. For our losses, his exchequer is too poor; for th' effusion of our blood, the muster of his Kingdom too faint a number; and for our disgrace, his own person kneeling at our feet, but a weak and worthless satisfaction. To this add defiance: and tell him for conclusion, he hath betrayed his followers, whose condemnation is pronounc'd: so far my King and master; so much my office.

KING HENRY: What is thy name? I know thy quality.

MONTJOY: Montjoy.

KING HENRY: Thou dost thy office fairly. Turn thee back,
And tell thy King, I do not seek him now,
But could be willing to march on to Callice,
Without impeachment: for to say the sooth,
Though 'tis no wisdom to confess so much
Unto an enemy of craft and vantage,
My people are with sickness much enfeebled,
My number lessen'd: and those few I have,
Almost no better than so many French;
Who when they were in health, I tell thee Herald,
I thought, upon one pair of English legs
Did march three Frenchmen. Yet forgive me God,
That I do brag thus; this your air of France
Hath blown that vice in me. I must repent:
Go therefore tell thy master, here I am;
My ransom, is this frail and worthless trunk;
My army, but a weak and sickly guard:
Yet God before, tell him we will come on,
Though France himself, and such another neighbour
Stand in our way. There's for thy labour Montjoy.
Go bid thy master well advise himself.
If we may pass, we will: if we be hinder'd,
We shall your tawny ground with your red blood

Discolour: and so Montjoy, fare you well.
The sum of all our answer is but this:
We would not seek a battle as we are,
Nor as we are, we say we will not shun it:
So tell your master.

MONTJOY: I shall deliver so: thanks to your Highness.

Exit.

GLOUCESTER: I hope they will not come upon us now.

KING HENRY: We are in God's hand, brother, not in theirs:
March to the bridge, it now draws toward night,
Beyond the river we'll encamp ourselves,
And on to-morrow bid them march away.

Exeunt.

III. 7

Enter the Constable of France, the Lord Rambures, Orleans, Dolphin, with others.

CONSTABLE: Tut, I have the best armour of the world: would it were day.

ORLEANS: You have an excellent armour: but let my horse have his due.

CONSTABLE: It is the best horse of Europe.

ORLEANS: Will it never be morning?

DOLPHIN: My Lord of Orleans, and my Lord High Constable, you talk of horse and armour?

ORLEANS: You are as well provided of both, as any Prince in the world.

DOLPHIN: What a long night is this? I will not change my horse with any that treads but on four pasterns: ch' ha: he bounds from the earth, as if his entrails were hairs: *le cheval volant*, the Pegasus, *chez les narines de feu*. When I bestride him, I soar, I am a hawk: he trots the air: the earth sings, when he touches it: the basest horn of his hoof, is more musical than the pipe of Hermes.

ORLEANS: He's of the colour of the nutmeg.

DOLPHIN: And of the heat of the ginger. It is a beast for Perseus: he is pure air and fire; and the dull elements of earth and water never appear in him, but only in patient stillness while his rider mounts him: he is indeed a horse, and all other jades you may call beasts.

CONSTABLE: Indeed my Lord, it is a most absolute and excellent horse.

DOLPHIN: It is the prince of palfreys, his neigh is like the bidding of a monarch, and his countenance enforces homage.

ORLEANS: No more cousin.

DOLPHIN: Nay, the man hath no wit, that cannot from the rising of the lark to the lodging of the lamb, vary deserved praise on my palfrey: it is a theme as fluent as the sea: turn the sands into eloquent tongues, and my horse is argument for them all: 'tis a subject for a sovereign to reason on, and for a sovereign's sovereign to ride on: and for the world, familiar to us, and unknown, to lay apart their particular functions, and wonder at him. I once writ a sonnet in his praise, and began thus, *Wonder of nature.*

ORLEANS: I have heard a sonnet begin so to one's mistress.

DOLPHIN: Then did they imitate that which I compos'd to my courser, for my horse is my mistress.

ORLEANS: Your mistress bears well.

DOLPHIN: Me well, which is the prescript praise and perfection of a good and particular mistress.

CONSTABLE: Nay, for methought yesterday your mistress shrewdly shook your back.

DOLPHIN: So perhaps did yours.

CONSTABLE: Mine was not bridled.

DOLPHIN: O then belike she was old and gentle, and you rode like a kern of Ireland, your French hose off, and in your strait strossers.

CONSTABLE: You have good judgement in horsemanship.

DOLPHIN: Be warn'd by me then: they that ride so, and ride not warily, fall into foul bogs: I had rather have my horse to my mistress.

CONSTABLE: I had as lief have my mistress a jade.

DOLPHIN: I tell thee Constable, my mistress wears his own hair.

CONSTABLE: I could make as true a boast as that, if I had a sow to my mistress.

DOLPHIN: *Le chien est retourné à son propre vomissement, et la truie lavée au bourbier*: thou mak'st use of any thing.

CONSTABLE: Yet do I not use my horse for my mistress, or any such proverb, so little kin to the purpose.

RAMBURES: My Lord Constable, the armour that I saw in your tent to-night, are those stars or suns upon it?

CONSTABLE: Stars, my Lord.

DOLPHIN: Some of them will fall to-morrow, I hope.

CONSTABLE: And yet my sky shall not want.

DOLPHIN: That may be, for you bear a many superfluously, and 'twere more honour some were away.

CONSTABLE: Even as your horse bears your praises, who would trot as well, were some of your brags dismounted.

DOLPHIN: Would I were able to load him with his desert. Will it never be day? I will trot to-morrow a mile, and my way shall be paved with English faces.

CONSTABLE: I will not say so, for fear I should be fac'd out of my way: but I would it were morning, for I would fain be about the ears of the English.

RAMBURES: Who will go to hazard with me for twenty prisoners?

CONSTABLE: You must first go yourself to hazard, ere you have them.

DOLPHIN: 'Tis midnight, I'll go arm myself.

Exit.

ORLEANS: The Dolphin longs for morning.

RAMBURES: He longs to eat the English.

CONSTABLE: I think he will eat all he kills.

ORLEANS: By the white hand of my Lady, he's a gallant Prince.

CONSTABLE: Swear by her foot, that she may tread out the oath.

ORLEANS: He is simply the most active gentleman of France.

CONSTABLE: Doing is activity, and he will still be doing.

ORLEANS: He never did harm, that I heard of.

CONSTABLE: Nor will do none to-morrow: he will keep that good name still.

ORLEANS: I know him to be valiant.

CONSTABLE: I was told that, by one that knows him better than you.

ORLEANS: What's he?

CONSTABLE: Marry he told me so himself, and he said he car'd not who knew it.

ORLEANS: He needs not, it is no hidden virtue in him.

CONSTABLE: By my faith, sir, but it is: never any body saw it, but his lackey: 'tis a hooded valour, and when it appears, it will bate.

ORLEANS: Ill will never said well.

CONSTABLE: I will cap that proverb with, There is flattery in friendship.

ORLEANS: And I will take up that with, Give the Devil his due.

CONSTABLE: Well plac'd: there stands your friend for

the Devil: have at the very eye of that proverb with, A pox of the Devil.

ORLEANS: You are the better at proverbs, by how much a fool's bolt is soon shot.

CONSTABLE: You have shot over.

ORLEANS: 'Tis not the first time you were overshot.

Enter a Messenger.

MESSENGER: My Lord High Constable, the English lie within fifteen hundred paces of your tents.

CONSTABLE: Who hath measur'd the ground?

MESSENGER: The Lord Grandpré.

CONSTABLE: A valiant and most expert gentleman. Would it were day! Alas poor Harry of England; he longs not for the dawning, as we do.

ORLEANS: What a wretched and peevish fellow is this King of England, to mope with his fat-brain'd followers so far out of his knowledge.

CONSTABLE: If the English had any apprehension, they would run away.

ORLEANS: That they lack: for if their heads had any intellectual armour, they could never wear such heavy head-pieces.

RAMBURES: That Island of England breeds very valiant creatures; their mastiffs are of unmatchable courage.

ORLEANS: Foolish curs, that run winking into the mouth of a Russian bear, and have their heads crush'd like rotten apples: you may as well say, that's a valiant flea, that dare eat his breakfast on the lip of a lion.

CONSTABLE: Just, just: and the men do sympathize with the mastiffs, in robustious and rough coming on, leaving their wits with their wives: and then give them great meals of beef, and iron and steel; they will eat like wolves, and fight like devils.

ORLEANS: Ay, but these English are shrewdly out of beef.

CONSTABLE: Then shall we find to-morrow, they have only stomachs to eat, and none to fight. Now is it time to arm: come, shall we about it?

ORLEANS: It is now two o'clock: but let me see, by ten
We shall have each a hundred Englishmen.

Exeunt.

IV

Chorus.

CHORUS: Now entertain conjecture of a time,
When creeping murmur and the poring dark
Fills the wide vessel of the Universe.
From camp to camp, through the foul womb of Night
The hum of either army stilly sounds;
That the fix'd sentinels almost receive
The secret whispers of each other's watch.
Fire answers fire, and through their paly flames
Each battle sees the other's umber'd face.
Steed threatens steed, in high and boastful neighs
Piercing the Night's dull ear: and from the tents,
The armourers accomplishing the Knights,
With busy hammers closing rivets up,
Give dreadful note of preparation.
The country cocks do crow, the clocks do toll:
And the third hour of drowsy morning name.
Proud of their numbers, and secure in soul,
The confident and over-lusty French,
Do the low-rated English play at dice;
And chide the cripple-tardy-gaited Night,
Who like a foul and ugly witch doth limp

So tediously away. The poor condemned English,
Like sacrifices, by their watchful fires
Sit patiently, and inly ruminate
The morning's danger: and their gesture sad,
Investing lank-lean cheeks, and war-worn coats,
Presenteth them unto the gazing Moon
So many horrid ghosts. O now, who will behold
The royal Captain of this ruin'd band
Walking from watch to watch, from tent to tent;
Let him cry, Praise and glory on his head:
For forth he goes, and visits all his host,
Bids them good morrow with a modest smile,
And calls them brothers, friends, and countrymen.
Upon his royal face there is no note,
How dread an army hath enrounded him;
Nor doth he dedicate one jot of colour
Unto the weary and all-watched Night:
But freshly looks, and over-bears attaint,
With cheerful semblance, and sweet majesty:
That ever wretch, pining and pale before,
Beholding him, plucks comfort from his looks.
A largess universal, like the sun,
His liberal eye doth give to every one,
Thawing cold fear, that mean and gentle all
Behold, as may unworthiness define,
A little touch of Harry in the night.
And so our scene must to the battle fly:
Where, O for pity, we shall much disgrace,
With four or five most vile and ragged foils,
(Right ill dispos'd, in brawl ridiculous)
The name of Agincourt: yet sit and see,
Minding true things, by what their mock'ries be.

Exit.

IV. I

Enter the King, Bedford, and Gloucester.

KING HENRY: Gloucester, 'tis true that we are in great danger,
The greater therefore should our courage be.
Good morrow brother Bedford: God Almighty,
There is some soul of goodness in things evil,
Would men observingly distil it out.
For our bad neighbour makes us early stirrers,
Which is both healthful, and good husbandry.
Besides, they are our outward consciences,
And preachers to us all; admonishing,
That we should dress us fairly for our end.
Thus may we gather honey from the weed,
And make a moral of the Devil himself.

Enter Erpingham.

Good morrow old Sir Thomas Erpingham:
A good soft pillow for that good white head,
Were better than a churlish turf of France.

ERPINGHAM: Not so my Liege, this lodging likes me better,
Since I may say, now lie I like a King.

KING HENRY: 'Tis good for men to love their present pains,
Upon example, so the spirit is eased:
And when the mind is quicken'd, out of doubt
The organs, though defunct and dead before,
Break up their drowsy grave, and newly move
With casted slough, and fresh legerity.
Lend me thy cloak Sir Thomas: brothers both,
Commend me to the Princes in our camp;
Do my good morrow to them, and anon
Desire them all to my pavilion.

GLOUCESTER: We shall, my Liege.

ERPINGHAM: Shall I attend your Grace?

KING HENRY: No, my good Knight:
Go with my brothers to my Lords of England:
I and my bosom must debate a while,
And then I would no other company.

ERPINGHAM: The Lord in Heaven bless thee, noble Harry.

Exeunt all but King.

KING HENRY: God-a-mercy old heart, thou speak'st cheerfully.

Enter Pistol.

PISTOL: *Che vous la?*

KING HENRY: A friend.

PISTOL: Discuss unto me, art thou officer, or art thou base, common, and popular?

KING HENRY: I am a gentleman of a company.

PISTOL: Trail'st thou the puissant pike?

KING HENRY: Even so: what are you?

PISTOL: As good a gentleman as the Emperor.

KING HENRY: Then you are a better than the King.

PISTOL: The King's a bawcock, and a heart of gold, a lad of life, an imp of fame, of parents good, of fist most valiant: I kiss his dirty shoe, and from heartstring I love the lovely bully. What is thy name?

KING HENRY: Harry le Roy.

PISTOL: Le Roy? a Cornish name: art thou of Cornish crew?

KING HENRY: No, I am a Welshman.

PISTOL: Know'st thou Fluellen?

KING HENRY: Yes.

PISTOL: Tell him I'll knock his leek about his pate upon Saint Davy's day.

KING HENRY: Do not you wear your dagger in your cap that day, lest he knock that about yours.

PISTOL: Art thou his friend?

KING HENRY: And his kinsman too.

PISTOL: The *figo* for thee then.

KING HENRY: I thank you: God be with you.

PISTOL: My name is Pistol call'd.

Exit.

KING HENRY: It sorts well with your fierceness.

Manet King.

Enter Fluellen and Gower.

GOWER: Captain Fluellen.

FLUELLEN: 'So, in the Name of Jesu Christ, speak fewer: it is the greatest admiration in the universal World, when the true and aunchient prerogatifes and laws of the wars is not kept: if you would take the pains but to examine the wars of Pompey the Great, you shall find, I warrant you, that there is no tiddle taddle nor pibble pabble in Pompey's camp: I warrant you, you shall find the ceremonies of the wars, and the cares of it, and the forms of it, and the sobriety of it, and the modesty of it, to be otherwise.

GOWER: Why the enemy is loud, you hear him all night.

FLUELLEN: If the enemy is an ass and a fool, and a prating coxcomb, is it meet, think you, that we should also. look you, be an ass and a fool, and a prating coxcomb, in your own conscience now?

GOWER: I will speak lower.

FLUELLEN: I pray you, and beseech you, that you will.

Exeunt Gower and Fluellen.

KING HENRY: Though it appear a little out of fashion,
There is much care and valour in this Welshman.

Enter three soldiers, John Bates, Alexander Court, and Michael Williams.

COURT: Brother John Bates, is not that the morning which breaks yonder?

BATES: I think it be: but we have no great cause to desire the approach of day.

WILLIAMS: We see yonder the beginning of the day, but I think we shall never see the end of it. Who goes there?

KING HENRY: A friend.

WILLIAMS: Under what Captain serve you?

KING HENRY: Under Sir Thomas Erpingham.

WILLIAMS: A good old commander, and a most kind gentleman: I pray you, what thinks he of our estate?

KING HENRY: Even as men wrack'd upon a sand, that look to be wash'd off the next tide.

BATES: He hath not told his thought to the King?

KING HENRY: No; nor it is not meet he should: for though I speak it to you, I think the King is but a man, as I am: the violet smells to him, as it doth to me; the element shows to him, as it doth to me; all his senses have but human conditions: his ceremonies laid by, in his nakedness he appears but a man; and though his affections are higher mounted than ours, yet when they stoop, they stoop with the like wing: therefore, when he sees reason of fears, as we do; his fears, out of doubt, be of the same relish as ours are: yet in reason, no man should possess him with any appearance of fear; lest he, by showing it, should dishearten his army.

BATES: He may show what outward courage he will: but I believe as cold a night as 'tis, he could wish himself in Thames up to the neck; and so I would he were, and I by him, at all adventures, so we were quit here.

KING HENRY: By my troth, I will speak my conscience of the King: I think he would not wish himself any where, but where he is.

BATES: Then I would he were here alone; so should he be sure to be ransomed, and a many poor men's lives saved.

KING HENRY: I dare say, you love him not so ill, to wish him here alone: howsoever you speak this to feel other men's minds, methinks I could not die any where so contented, as in the King's company; his cause being just, and his quarrel honourable.

WILLIAMS: That's more than we know.

BATES: Ay, or more than we should seek after; for we know enough, if we know we are the King's subjects: if his cause be wrong, our obedience to the King wipes the crime of it out of us.

WILLIAMS: But if the cause be not good, the King himself hath a heavy reckoning to make, when all those legs, and arms, and heads, chopped off in a battle, shall join together at the latter day, and cry all, We died at such a place, some swearing, some crying for a surgeon; some upon their wives, left poor behind them; some upon the debts they owe, some upon their children rawly left: I am afear'd, there are few die well, that die in a battle: for how can they charitably dispose of any thing, when blood is their argument? Now, if these men do not die well, it will be a black matter for the King, that led them to it; whom to disobey, were against all proportion of subjection.

KING HENRY: So, if a son that is by his father sent about merchandise, do sinfully miscarry upon the sea; the imputation of his wickedness, by your rule, should be imposed upon his father that sent him: or if a servant, under his master's command, transporting a sum of money, be assail'd by robbers, and die in many irreconcil'd iniquities; you may call the business of the master the author of the servant's damnation: but this is not so: the King is not bound to answer the particular endings of his soldiers, the father of his son, nor the master of his servant; for they purpose not their death, when they purpose their services. Besides, there is no King, be his cause never so spotless, if it come to the arbitrement of swords, can try it out with all unspotted soldiers: some (peradventure) have on them the guilt of premeditated and contrived murther; some, of beguiling virgins with the broken seals of perjury; some, making the wars their bulwark, that have before gored the gentle bosom of peace with pillage and robbery. Now, if these men have defeated the Law, and outrun native punishment; though they can outstrip men, they have no wings to fly from God. War is his beadle; war is his vengeance: so that here men are punish'd, for before-breach of the King's Laws, in now the King's quarrel: where they feared the death, they have borne life away; and where they would be safe, they perish. Then if they die unprovided, no more is the King guilty of their damnation, than he was before guilty of those impieties, for the which they are now visited. Every subject's duty is the King's, but every subject's soul is his own. Therefore should every soldier in the wars do as every sick man in his bed, wash every moth out of his conscience: and dying so, death is to him advantage; or not dying, the time was blessedly lost, wherein such preparation was gained: and in him that escapes, it were not sin to think, that making God so free an offer, he let him outlive that day, to see his Greatness, and to teach others how they should prepare.

WILLIAMS: 'Tis certain, every man that dies ill, the ill upon his own head, the King is not to answer it.

BATES: I do not desire he should answer for me, and yet I determine to fight lustily for him.

KING HENRY: I myself heard the King say he would not be ransom'd.

WILLIAMS: Ay, he said so, to make us fight cheerfully: but when our throats are cut, he may be ransom'd, and we ne'er the wiser.

KING HENRY: If I live to see it, I will never trust his word after.

WILLIAMS: You pay him then: that's a perilous shot out of an elder-gun, that a poor and a private displeasure can do against a monarch: you may as well go about to turn the sun to ice, with fanning in his face with a peacock's feather: you'll never trust his word after; come, 'tis a foolish saying.

KING HENRY: Your reproof is something too round, I should be angry with you, if the time were convenient.

WILLIAMS: Let it be a quarrel between us, if you live.

KING HENRY: I embrace it.

WILLIAMS: How shall I know thee again?

KING HENRY: Give me any gage of thine, and I will wear it in my bonnet: then if ever thou darest acknowledge it, I will make it my quarrel.

WILLIAMS: Here's my glove: give me another of thine.

KING HENRY: There.

WILLIAMS: This will I also wear in my cap: if ever thou come to me, and say, after to-morrow, This is my glove, by this hand I will take thee a box on the ear.

KING HENRY: If ever I live to see it, I will challenge it.

WILLIAMS: Thou darest as well be hang'd.

KING HENRY: Well, I will do it, though I take thee in the King's company.

WILLIAMS: Keep thy word: fare thee well.

BATES: Be friends you English fools, be friends, we have French quarrels enow, if you could tell how to reckon.

KING HENRY: Indeed the French may lay twenty French crowns to one, they will beat us, for they bear them on their shoulders: but it is no English treason to cut French crowns, and to-morrow the King himself will be a clipper.

Exeunt Soldiers.

Upon the King, let us our lives, our souls,
Our debts, our careful wives,
Our children, and our sins, lay on the King:
We must bear all.
O hard condition, twin-born with greatness,
Subject to the breath of every fool, whose sense
No more can feel, but his own wringing.
What infinite heart's-ease must Kings neglect,
That private men enjoy?
And what have Kings, that privates have not too,
Save ceremony, save general ceremony?
And what art thou, thou idol ceremony?
What kind of god art thou? that suffer'st more
Of mortal griefs, than do thy worshippers.
What are thy rents? what are thy comings in?
O ceremony, show me but thy worth.
What? is thy soul of adoration?
Art thou aught else but place, degree, and form,
Creating awe and fear in other men?
Wherein thou art less happy, being fear'd,
Than they in fearing.
What drink'st thou oft, instead of homage sweet,
But poison'd flattery? O, be sick, great greatness,
And bid thy ceremony give thee cure.
Think'st thou the fiery fever will go out
With titles blown from adulation?

Will it give place to flexure and low bending?
Canst thou, when thou command'st the beggar's knee,
Command the health of it: No, thou proud dream,
That play'st so subtly with a King's repose.
I am a King that find thee: and I know,
'Tis not the balm, the sceptre, and the ball,
The sword, the mace, the crown imperial,
The intertissued robe of gold and pearl,
The farced title running 'fore the King,
The throne he sits on: nor the tide of pomp,
That beats upon the high shore of this world:
No, not all these, thrice-gorgeous ceremony;
Not all these, laid in bed majestical,
Can sleep so soundly, as the wretched slave:
Who with a body fill'd, and vacant mind,
Gets him to rest, cramm'd with distressful bread,
Never sees horrid night, the child of Hell:
But like a lackey, from the rise to set,
Sweats in the eye of Phœbus; and all night
Sleeps in Elysium: next day after dawn,
Doth rise and help Hyperion to his horse,
And follows so the ever-running year
With profitable labour to his grave:
And but for ceremony, such a wretch,
Winding up days with toil, and nights with sleep,
Had the fore-hand and vantage of a King.
The slave, a member of the country's peace,
Enjoys it; but in gross brain little wots,
What watch the King keeps, to maintain the peace;
Whose hours, the peasant best advantages.

Enter Erpingham.

ERPINGHAM: My Lord, your Nobles jealous of your absence,

Seek through the camp to find you.

KING HENRY: Good old Knight, collect them all together
At my tent: I'll be before thee.

ERPINGHAM: I shall do't, my Lord.

Exit.

KING HENRY: O God of battles, steel my soldiers' hearts,
Possess them not with fear: take from them now
The sense of reckoning of th' opposed numbers:
Pluck their hearts from them. Not to-day, O Lord,
O not to-day, think not upon the fault
My father made, in compassing the crown.
I Richard's body have interred new,
And on it have bestow'd more contrite tears,
Than from it issued forced drops of blood.
Five hundred poor I have in yearly pay,
Who twice a-day their wither'd hands hold up
Toward Heaven, to pardon blood:
And I have built two chantries,
Where the sad and solemn priests sing still
For Richard's soul. More will I do:
Though all that I can do, is nothing worth;
Since that my penitence comes after all,
Imploring pardon.

Enter Gloucester.

GLOUCESTER: My Liege.

KING HENRY: My brother Gloucester's voice? Ay:
I know thy errand, I will go with thee:
The day, my friends, and all things stay for me.

Exeunt.

IV.2

Enter the Dolphin, Orleans, Rambures, and Beaumont.

ORLEANS: The sun doth gild our armour, up my Lords.

DOLPHIN: *Monte cheval*: My horse, *varlet, laquais:* ha.

ORLEANS: Oh brave spirit.

DOLPHIN: *Via, les eaux et la terre.*

ORLEANS: *Rien puis? l'air et le feu.*

DOLPHIN: *Ciel*, cousin Orleans.

Enter Constable.

Now my Lord Constable?

CONSTABLE: Hark how our steeds, for present service neigh.

DOLPHIN: Mount them, and make incision in their hides,
That their hot blood may spin in English eyes,
And dout them with superfluous courage: ha.

RAMBURES: What, will you have them weep our horses' blood?
How shall we then behold their natural tears?

Enter Messenger.

MESSENGER: The English are embattl'd, you French Peers.

CONSTABLE: To horse you gallant Princes, straight to horse.
Do but behold yond poor and starved band,
And your fair show shall suck away their souls,
Leaving them but the shales and husks of men.
There is not work enough for all our hands,
Scarce blood enough in all their sickly veins,
To give each naked curtle-axe a stain,
That our French gallants shall to-day draw out,
And sheathe for lack of sport. Let us but blow on them,
The vapour of our valour will o'erturn them.

'Tis positive 'gainst all exceptions, Lords,
That our superfluous lackeys, and our peasants,
Who in unnecessary action swarm
About our squares of battle, were enow
To purge this field of such a hilding foe;
Though we upon this mountain's basis by,
Took stand for idle speculation:
But that our honours must not. What's to say?
A very little little let us do,
And all is done: then let the trumpets sound
The tucket sonance, and the note to mount:
For our approach shall so much dare the field,
That England shall couch down in fear, and yield.

Enter Grandpré.

GRANDPRÉ: Why do you stay so long, my Lords of France?
Yond island carrions, desperate of their bones,
Ill-favouredly become the morning field;
Their ragged curtains poorly are let loose,
And our air shakes them passing scornfully.
Big Mars seems bankrout in their beggar'd host,
And faintly through a rusty beaver peeps.
The horsemen sit like fixed candlesticks,
With torch-staves in their hand: and their poor jades
Lob down their heads, dropping the hides and hips:
The gum down-roping from their pale-dead eyes,
And in their pale dull mouths the gimmal bit
Lies foul with chaw'd grass, still and motionless.
And their executors, the knavish crows,
Fly o'er them all, impatient for their hour.
Description cannot suit itself in words,
To demonstrate the life of such a battle,
In life so lifeless, as it shows itself.

CONSTABLE: They have said their prayers,

And they stay for death.

DOLPHIN: Shall we go send them dinners, and fresh suits,
And give their fasting horses provender,
And after fight with them?

CONSTABLE: I stay but for my guard: on
To the field, I will the banner from a trumpet take,
And use it for my haste. Come, come away.
The sun is high, and we outwear the day.

Exeunt.

IV. 3

Enter Gloucester, Bedford, Exeter, Erpingham, with all his host; Salisbury and Westmoreland.

GLOUCESTER: Where is the King?

BEDFORD: The King himself is rode to view their battle.

WESTMORELAND: Of fighting men they have full three score thousand.

EXETER: There's five to one, besides they all are fresh.

SALISBURY: God's arm strike with us, 'tis a fearful odds.
God be wi' you Princes all; I'll to my charge:
If we no more meet, till we meet in Heaven;
Then joyfully, my noble Lord of Bedford,
My dear Lord Gloucester, and my good Lord Exeter,
And my kind kinsman, warriors all, adieu.

BEDFORD: Farewell good Salisbury, and good luck go with thee:
And yet I do thee wrong, to mind thee of it,
For thou art fram'd of the firm truth of valour.

EXETER: Farewell kind Lord: fight valiantly to-day.

Exit Salisbury.

BEDFORD: He is as full of valour as of kindness,
Princely in both.

Enter the King.

WESTMORELAND: O that we now had here
But one ten thousand of those men in England,
That do no work to-day.

KING HENRY: What's he that wishes so?
My cousin Westmoreland. No, my fair cousin:
If we are mark'd to die, we are enow
To do our country loss: and if to live,
The fewer men, the greater share of honour.
God's will, I pray thee wish not one man more.
By Jove, I am not covetous for gold,
Nor care I who doth feed upon my cost:
It yearns me not, if men my garments wear:
Such outward things dwell not in my desires.
But if it be a sin to covet honour,
I am the most offending soul alive.
No 'faith, my coz, wish not a man from England:
God's peace, I would not lose so great an honour,
As one man more methinks would share from me,
For the best hope I have. O, do not wish one more:
Rather proclaim it, Westmoreland, through my host,
That he which hath no stomach to this fight,
Let him depart, his passport shall be made,
And crowns for convoy put into his purse:
We would not die in that man's company,
That fears his fellowship, to die with us.
This day is call'd the Feast of Crispian:
He that outlives this day, and comes safe home,
Will stand a tip-toe when this day is named,
And rouse him at the name of Crispian.
He that shall live this day, and see old age,
Will yearly on the Vigil feast his neighbours,
And say, to-morrow is Saint Crispian.

Then will he strip his sleeve, and show his scars:
Old men forget; yet all shall be forgot:
But he'll remember, with advantages,
What feats he did that day. Then shall our names,
Familiar in his mouth as household words,
Harry the King, Bedford and Exeter,
Warwick and Talbot, Salisbury and Gloucester,
Be in their flowing cups freshly remember'd.
This story shall the good man teach his son:
And Crispin Crispian shall ne'er go by,
From this day to the ending of the World,
But we in it shall be remembered:
We few, we happy few, we band of brothers:
For he to-day that sheds his blood with me,
Shall be my brother: be he ne'er so vile,
This day shall gentle his condition.
And gentlemen in England, now a-bed,
Shall think themselves accurs'd they were not here;
And hold their manhoods cheap, whiles any speaks,
That fought with us upon Saint Crispin's day.

Enter Salisbury.

SALISBURY: My Sovereign Lord, bestow yourself with speed:
The French are bravely in their battles set,
And will with all expedience charge on us.

KING HENRY: All things are ready, if our minds be so.

WESTMORELAND: Perish the man, whose mind is backward now.

KING HENRY: Thou dost not wish more help from England, coz?

WESTMORELAND: God's will, my Liege, would you and I alone,
Without more help, could fight this royal battle.

KING HENRY: Why now thou hast unwish'd five thousand men:
Which likes me better, than to wish us one.
You know your places: God be with you all.

Tucket. Enter Montjoy.

MONTJOY: Once more I come to know of thee King Harry,
If for thy ransom thou wilt now compound,
Before thy most assured overthrow:
For certainly, thou art so near the gulf,
Thou needs must be englutted. Besides, in mercy
The Constable desires thee, thou wilt mind
Thy followers of repentance; that their souls
May make a peaceful and a sweet retire
From off these fields: where (wretches) their poor bodies
Must lie and fester.

KING HENRY: Who hath sent thee now?

MONTJOY: The Constable of France.

KING HENRY: I pray thee bear my former answer back:
Bid them achieve me, and then sell my bones.
Good God, why should they mock poor fellows thus?
The man that once did sell the lion's skin
While the beast liv'd, was kill'd with hunting him.
A many of our bodies shall no doubt
Find native graves: upon the which, I trust
Shall witness live in brass of this day's work.
And those that leave their valiant bones in France,
Dying like men, though buried in your dunghills,
They shall be fam'd: for there the sun shall greet them,
And draw their honours reeking up to Heaven,
Leaving their earthly parts to choke your clime,
The smell whereof shall breed a plague in France.
Mark then abounding valour in our English:
That being dead, like to the bullet's crazing,

Break out into a second course of mischief,
Killing in relapse of mortality.
Let me speak proudly: tell the Constable,
We are but warriors for the working day:
Our gayness and our gilt are all besmirch'd
With rainy marching in the painful field.
There's not a piece of feather in our host:
Good argument (I hope) we will not fly:
And time hath worn us into slovenry.
But by the Mass, our hearts are in the trim:
And my poor soldiers tell me, yet ere night,
They'll be in fresher robes, or they will pluck
The gay new coats o'er the French soldiers' heads,
And turn them out of service. If they do this,
As, if God please, they shall; my ransom then
Will soon be levied.
Herald, save thou thy labour:
Come thou no more for ransom, gentle Herald,
They shall have none, I swear, but these my joints:
Which if they have, as I will leave 'em them,
Shall yield them little, tell the Constable.

MONTJOY: I shall, King Harry. And so fare thee well:
Thou never shalt hear Herald any more.

Exit,

KING HENRY: I fear thou'lt once more come again for ransom.

Enter York.

YORK: My Lord, most humbly on my knee I beg
The leading of the vaward.

KING HENRY: Take it, brave York.
Now soldiers march away,
And how thou pleasest God, dispose the day.

Exeunt.

IV.4

Alarum. Excursions.

Enter Pistol, French Soldier, and Boy.

PISTOL: Yield cur.

FRENCH SOLDIER: *Je pense que vous êtes le gentilhomme de bonne qualité.*

PISTOL: Qualtitie calmie custure me. Art thou a gentleman? What is thy name? discuss.

FRENCH SOLDIER: O *Seigneur Dieu.*

PISTOL: O Signieur Dew should be a gentleman: perpend my words O Signieur Dew, and mark: O Signieur Dew, thou diest on point of fox, except O Signieur thou do give to me egregious ransom.

FRENCH SOLDIER: *O, prenez miséricorde, ayez pitié de moi.*

PISTOL: Moy shall not serve, I will have forty moys: for I will fetch thy rim out at thy throat, in drops of crimson blood.

FRENCH SOLDIER: *Est-il impossible d'échapper la force de ton bras?*

PISTOL: Brass, cur? Thou damned and luxurious mountain goat, offer'st me brass?

FRENCH SOLDIER: O *pardonnez moi.*

PISTOL: Say'st thou me so? is that a ton of moys? Come hither boy, ask me this slave in French what is his name.

BOY: *Ecoutez: comment êtes-vous appelé?*

FRENCH SOLDIER: *Monsieur le Fer.*

BOY: He says his name is Master Fer.

PISTOL: Master Fer: I'll fer him, and firk him, and ferret him: discuss the same in French unto him.

BOY: I do not know the French for fer, and ferret, and firk.

PISTOL: Bid him prepare, for I will cut his throat.

FRENCH SOLDIER: *Que dit-il, monsieur?*

BOY: *Il me commande de vous dire que vous faites vous prêt, car ce soldat ici est disposé tout à cette heure de couper votre gorge.*

PISTOL: Owy, cuppele gorge permafoy peasant, unless thou give me crowns, brave crowns; or mangled shalt thou be by this my sword.

FRENCH SOLDIER: *O je vous supplie, pour l'amour de Dieu: me pardonner, je suis gentilhomme de bonne maison, gardez ma vie, et je vous donnerai deux cents écus.*

PISTOL: What are his words?

BOY: He prays you to save his life, he is a gentleman of a good house, and for his ransom he will give you two hundred crowns.

PISTOL: Tell him my fury shall abate, and I the crowns will take.

FRENCH SOLDIER: *Petit monsieur, que dit-il?*

BOY: *Encore qu'il est contre son jurement de pardonner aucun prisonnier. Néanmoins pour les écus que vous l'avez promis, il est content de vous donner la liberté, le franchisement.*

FRENCH SOLDIER: *Sur mes genoux je vous donne mille remercîmens, et je m'estime heureux que je suis tombé entre les mains d'un chevalier, je pense, le plus brave, vaillant, et très distingué seigneur d'Angleterre.*

PISTOL: Expound unto me boy.

BOY: He gives you upon his knees a thousand thanks, and he esteems himself happy, that he hath fallen into the hands of one (as he thinks) the most brave, valorous and thrice-worthy signieur of England.

PISTOL: As I suck blood, I will some mercy show. Follow me.

BOY: *Suivez-vous le grand capitaine!*

Exeunt Pistol, and French Soldier.

I did never know so full a voice issue from so empty a heart: but the saying is true, The empty vessel makes the greatest sound. Bardolph and Nym had ten times more valour, than this roaring devil i' th' old play, that every one may pare his nails with a wooden dagger, and they are both hang'd, and so would this be, if he durst steal any thing adventurously. I must stay with the lackeys with the luggage of our camp; the French might have a good prey of us, if he knew of it, for there is none to guard it but boys.

Exit.

IV.5

Enter Constable, Orleans, Bourbon, Dolphin, and Rambures.

CONSTABLE: O *diable.*

ORLEANS: O *seigneur, le jour est perdu, tout est perdu.*

DOLPHIN: *Mort de ma vie,* all is confounded all,
Reproach, and everlasting shame
Sits mocking in our plumes.

A short alarum.

O *méchante fortune,* do not run away.

CONSTABLE: Why all our ranks are broke.

DOLPHIN: O perdurable shame, let's stab ourselves:
Be these the wretches that we play'd at dice for?

ORLEANS: Is this the King we sent to, for his ransom?

BOURBON: Shame, and eternal shame, nothing but shame,
Let us die in honour: once more back again,
And he that will not follow Bourbon now,
Let him go hence, and with his cap in hand
Like a base pandar hold the chamber-door,
Whilst by a slave, no gentler than my dog,
His fairest daughter is contaminated.

CONSTABLE: Disorder that hath spoil'd us, friend us now,
Let us on heaps go offer up our lives.

ORLEANS: We are enow yet living in the field,
To smother up the English in our throngs,
If any order might be thought upon.

BOURBON: The devil take order now, I'll to the throng;
Let life be short, else shame will be too long.

Exeunt.

IV.6

Alarum. Enter the King and his train, with prisoners.

KING HENRY: Well have we done, thrice valiant country-men,
But all's not done, yet keep the French the field.

EXETER: The Duke of York commends him to your Majesty.

KING HENRY: Lives he good uncle? thrice within this hour
I saw him down; thrice up again, and fighting,
From helmet to the spur, all blood he was.

EXETER: In which array (brave soldier) doth he lie,
Larding the plain: and by his bloody side,
(Yoke-fellow to his honour-owing wounds)
The noble Earl of Suffolk also lies.
Suffolk first died, and York all haggled over
Comes to him, where in gore he lay insteep'd,
And takes him by the beard, kisses the gashes
That bloodily did yawn upon his face.
And cries aloud; Tarry my cousin Suffolk,
My soul shall thine keep company to heaven:
Tarry (sweet soul) for mine, then fly abreast:
As in this glorious and well-foughten field
We kept together in our chivalry.

Upon these words I came, and cheer'd him up,
He smil'd me in the face, raught me his hand,
And with a feeble gripe, says: Dear my Lord,
Commend my service to my Sovereign,
So did he turn, and over Suffolk's neck
He threw his wounded arm, and kiss'd his lips,
And so espous'd to death, with blood he seal'd
A testament of noble-ending love:
The pretty and sweet manner of it forc'd
Those waters from me, which I would have stopp'd,
But I had not so much of man in me,
And all my mother came into mine eyes,
And gave me up to tears.

KING HENRY: I blame you not,
For hearing this, I must perforce compound
With mistful eyes, or they will issue too.

Alarum.

But hark, what new alarum is this same?
The French have reinforc'd their scatter'd men:
Then every soldier kill his prisoners,
Give the word through.

Exeunt.

IV. 7

Enter Fluellen and Gower.

FLUELLEN: Kill the poys and the luggage, 'tis expressly against the law of arms, 'tis as arrant a piece of knavery mark you now, as can be offer't in your conscience now, is it not?

GOWER: 'Tis certain, there's not a boy left alive, and the cowardly rascals that ran from the battle ha' done this slaughter: besides they have burned and carried away all that was in the King's tent, wherefore the King most worthily hath caus'd every soldier to cut his prisoner's throat. O 'tis a gallant King.

FLUELLEN: Ay, he was porn at Monmouth Captain Gower: what call you the town's name where Alexander the Pig was born?

GOWER: Alexander the Great.

FLUELLEN: Why I pray you, is not pig, great? the pig, or the great, or the mighty, or the huge, or the magnanimous, are all one reckonings, save the phrase is a little variations.

GOWER: I think Alexander the Great was born in Macedon, his father was called Philip of Macedon, as I take it.

FLUELLEN: I think it is in Macedon where Alexander is porn: I tell you Captain, if you look in the maps of the 'Orld, I warrant you sall find in the comparisons between Macedon and Monmouth, that the situations look you, is both alike. There is a river in Macedon, and there is also moreover a river at Monmouth, it is call'd Wye at Monmouth: but it is out of my prains, what is the name of the other river: but 'tis all one, 'tis alike as my fingers is to my fingers, and there is salmons in both. If you mark Alexander's life well, Harry of Monmouth's life is come after it indifferent well, for there is figures in all things. Alexander God knows, and you know, in his rages, and his furies, and his wraths, and his cholers, and his moods, and his displeasures, and his indignations, and also being a little intoxicates in his prains, did in his ales and his angers (look you) kill his best friend Cleitus.

GOWER: Our King is not like him in that, he never killed any of his friends.

FLUELLEN: It is not well done (mark you now) to take the tales out of my mouth, ere it is made and finished. I speak but in the figures, and comparisons of it: as

Alexander killed his friend Cleitus, being in his ales and his cups; so also Harry Monmouth being in his right wits, and his good judgements, turn'd away the fat Knight with the great-belly doublet: he was full of jests, and gipes, and knaveries, and mocks, I have forgot his name.

GOWER: Sir John Falstaff.

FLUELLEN: That is he: I'll tell you, there is good men porn at Monmouth.

GOWER: Here comes his Majesty.

Alarum. Enter King Henry, and Bourbon with prisoners, Warwick, Gloucester, Exeter. Flourish.

KING HENRY: I was not angry since I came to France,
Until this instant. Take a trumpet Herald,
Ride thou unto the horsemen on yond hill:
If they will fight with us, bid them come down,
Or void the field: they do offend our sight.
If they'll do neither, we will come to them,
And make them skirr away, as swift as stones
Enforced from the old Assyrian slings:
Besides, we'll cut the throats of those we have,
And not a man of them that we shall take,
Shall taste our mercy. Go and tell them so.

Enter Montjoy.

EXETER: Here comes the Herald of the French, my Liege.

GLOUCESTER: His eyes are humbler than they us'd to be.

KING HENRY: How now, what means this Herald?
Know'st thou not,
That I have fin'd these bones of mine for ransom?
Comest thou again for ransom?

MONTJOY: No great King:
I come to thee for charitable license,
That we may wander o'er this bloody field,
To book our dead, and then to bury them,

To sort our Nobles from our common men.
For many of our Princes (woe the while)
Lie drown'd and soak'd in mercenary blood:
So do our vulgar drench their peasant limbs
In blood of Princes, and their wounded steeds
Fret fetlock deep in gore, and with wild rage
Yerk out their armed heels at their dead masters,
Killing them twice. O give us leave great King,
To view the field in safety, and dispose
Of their dead bodies.

KING HENRY: I tell thee truly Herald,
I know not if the day be ours or no,
For yet a many of your horsemen peer,
And gallop o'er the field.

MONTJOY: The day is yours.

KING HENRY: Praised be God, and not our strength for it:
What is this Castle call'd that stands hard by?

MONTJOY: They call it Agincourt.

KING HENRY: Then call we this the field of Agincourt,
Fought on the day of Crispin Crispianus.

FLUELLEN: Your grandfather of famous memory (an 't please your Majesty) and your great-uncle Edward the Plack Prince of Wales, as I have read in the Chronicles, fought a most prave pattle here in France.

KING HENRY: They did Fluellen.

FLUELLEN: Your Majesty says very true; if your Majesties is remembered of it, the Welshmen did good service in a garden where leeks did grow, wearing leeks in their Monmouth caps, which your Majesty know to this hour is an honourable badge of the service: and I do believe your Majesty takes no scorn to wear the leek upon Saint Tavy's day.

KING HENRY: I wear it for a memorable honour:

For I am Welsh you know good countryman.

FLUELLEN: All the water in Wye, cannot wash your Majesty's Welsh plood out of your pody, I can tell you that: God pless it, and preserve it, as long as it pleases his Grace, and his Majesty too.

KING HENRY: Thanks good my countryman.

FLUELLEN: By Jeshu, I am your Majesty's countryman, I care not who know it: I will confess it to all the 'Orld, I need not to be ashamed of your Majesty, praised be God so long as your Majesty is an honest man.

KING HENRY: God keep me so.

Enter Williams.

Our Heralds go with him,
Bring me just notice of the numbers dead
On both our parts.

Exeunt Heralds with Montjoy.

Call yonder fellow hither.

EXETER: Soldier, you must come to the King.

KING HENRY: Soldier, why wear'st thou that glove in thy cap?

WILLIAMS: And 't please your Majesty, 'tis the gage of one that I should fight withal, if he be alive.

KING HENRY: An Englishman?

WILLIAMS: And 't please your Majesty, a rascal that swagger'd with me last night: who if alive, and ever dare to challenge this glove, I have sworn to take him a box a' th' ear: or if I can see my glove in his cap, which he swore as he was a soldier he would wear (if alive) I will strike it out soundly.

KING HENRY: What think you Captain Fluellen, is it fit this soldier keep his oath?

FLUELLEN: He is a craven and a villain else, and 't please your Majesty in my conscience.

KING HENRY: It may be, his enemy is a gentleman of great sort quite from the answer of his degree.

FLUELLEN: Though he be as good a gentleman as the devil is, as Lucifer and Belzebub himself, it is necessary (look your Grace) that he keep his vow and his oath: if he be perjur'd (see you now) his reputation is as arrant a villain and a Jacksauce, as ever his black shoe trod upon God's ground, and his earth, in my conscience law.

KING HENRY: Then keep thy vow sirrah, when thou meet'st the fellow.

WILLIAMS: So, I will my Liege, as I live.

KING HENRY: Who servest thou under?

WILLIAMS: Under Captain Gower, my Liege.

FLUELLEN: Gower is a good captain, and is good knowledge and literatured in the wars.

KING HENRY: Call him hither to me, soldier.

WILLIAMS: I will my Liege.

Exit.

KING HENRY: Here Fluellen, wear thou this favour for me, and stick it in thy cap: when Alanson and myself were down together, I pluck'd this glove from his helm: if any man challenge this, he is a friend to Alanson, and an enemy to our person; if thou encounter any such, apprehend him, and thou dost me love.

FLUELLEN: Your Grace doo's me as great honours as can be desir'd in the hearts of his subjects: I would fain see the man, that has but two legs, that shall find himself aggriefed at this glove; that is all: but I would fain see it once, and please God of his grace that I might see.

KING HENRY: Knowest thou Gower?

FLUELLEN: He is my dear friend, and please you.

KING HENRY: Pray thee go seek him, and bring him to my tent.

FLUELLEN: I will fetch him.

Exit.

KING HENRY: My Lord of Warwick, and my brother Gloucester,
Follow Fluellen closely at the heels.
The glove which I have given him for a favour,
May haply purchase him a box a' th' ear.
It is the soldier's: I by bargain should
Wear it myself. Follow good cousin Warwick:
If that the soldier strike him, as I judge
By his blunt bearing, he will keep his word;
Some sudden mischief may arise of it:
For I do know Fluellen valiant,
And touch'd with choler, hot as gunpowder,
And quickly will return an injury.
Follow, and see there be no harm between them.
Go you with me, uncle of Exeter.

Exeunt.

IV. 8

Enter Gower and Williams.

WILLIAMS: I warrant it is to knight you, Captain.

Enter Fluellen.

FLUELLEN: God's will, and his pleasure, Captain, I beseech you now, come apace to the King: there is more good toward you peradventure, than is in your knowledge to dream of.

WILLIAMS: Sir, know you this glove?

FLUELLEN: Know the glove? I know the glove is a glove.

WILLIAMS: I know this, and thus I challenge it.

Strikes him.

FLUELLEN: 'Sblood, an arrant traitor as any is in the universal World, or in France, or in England.

GOWER: How now sir? you villain.

WILLIAMS: Do you think I'll be forsworn?

FLUELLEN: Stand away Captain Gower, I will give treason his payment into plows, I warrant you.

WILLIAMS: I am no traitor.

FLUELLEN: That's a lie in thy throat. I charge you in his Majesty's name apprehend him, he's a friend of the Duke of Alanson's.

Enter Warwick and Gloucester.

WARWICK: How now, how now, what's the matter?

FLUELLEN: My Lord of Warwick, here is, praised be God for it, a most contagious treason come to light, look you, as you shall desire in a summer's day. Here is his Majesty.

Enter King and Exeter.

KING HENRY: How now, what's the matter?

FLUELLEN: My Liege, here is a villain, and a traitor, that look your Grace, has struck the glove which your Majesty is take out of the helmet of Alanson.

WILLIAMS: My Liege, this was my glove, here is the fellow of it: and he that I gave it to in change, promis'd to wear it in his cap: I promis'd to strike him, if he did; I met this man with my glove in his cap, and I have been as good as my word.

FLUELLEN: Your Majesty hear now, saving your Majesty's manhood, what an arrant rascally, beggarly, lousy knave it is: I hope your Majesty is pear me testimony and witness, and will avouchment, that this is the glove of Alanson, that your Majesty is give me, in your conscience now.

KING HENRY: Give me thy glove soldier;
Look, here is the fellow of it:

'Twas I indeed thou promised'st to strike,
And thou hast given me most bitter terms.

FLUELLEN: And please your Majesty, let his neck answer for it, if there is any martial law in the world.

KING HENRY: How canst thou make me satisfaction?

WILLIAMS: All offences, my Lord, come from the heart: never came any from mine, that might offend your Majesty.

KING HENRY: It was ourself thou didst abuse.

WILLIAMS: Your Majesty came not like yourself: you appear'd to me but as a common man; witness the night, your garments, your lowliness: and what your Highness suffer'd under that shape, I beseech you take it for your own fault, and not mine: for had you been as I took you for, I made no offence; therefore I beseech your Highness pardon me.

KING HENRY: Here uncle Exeter, fill this glove with crowns,
And give it to this fellow. Keep it fellow,
And wear it for an honour in thy cap,
Till I do challenge it. Give him the crowns:
And Captain, you must needs be friends with him.

FLUELLEN: By this day and this light, the fellow has mettle enough in his belly: hold, there is twelve pence for you, and I pray you to serve God, and keep you out of prawls and prabbles, and quarrels and dissensions, and I warrant you it is the better for you.

WILLIAMS: I will none of your money.

FLUELLEN: It is with a good will: I can tell you it will serve you to mend your shoes: come, wherefore should you be so pashful, your shoes is not so good: 'tis a good shilling I warrant you, or I will change it.

Enter Herald.

KING HENRY: Now Herald, are the dead number'd?

HERALD: Here is the number of the slaughter'd French.
KING HENRY: What prisoners of good sort are taken, uncle?
EXETER: Charles Duke of Orleans, nephew to the King,
John Duke of Bourbon, and Lord Bouciqualt:
Of other Lords and Barons, Knights and Squires,
Full fifteen hundred, besides common men.
KING HENRY: This note doth tell me of ten thousand French
That in the field lie slain: of Princes in this number,
And Nobles bearing banners, there lie dead
One hundred twenty six: added to these,
Of Knights, Esquires, and gallant gentlemen,
Eight thousand and four hundred: of the which,
Five hundred were but yesterday dubb'd Knights.
So that in these ten thousand they have lost,
There are but sixteen hundred mercenaries:
The rest are Princes, Barons, Lords, Knights, Squires,
And gentlemen of blood and quality.
The names of those their Nobles that lie dead:
Charles Delabreth, High Constable of France,
Jacques of Chatillon, Admiral of France,
The Master of the Cross-bows, Lord Rambures,
Great Master of France, the brave Sir Guichard Dolphin.
John Duke of Alanson, Anthony Duke of Brabant,
The brother to the Duke of Burgundy,
And Edward Duke of Bar: of lusty Earls,
Grandpré and Roussi, Falconbridge and Foix,
Beaumont and Marle, Vaudemont and Lestrale.
Here was a royal fellowship of death.
Where is the number of our English dead?
Edward the Duke of York, the Earl of Suffolk,
Sir Richard Ketly, Davy Gam, Esquire;
None else of name: and of all other men,

But five and twenty.
O God, Thy arm was here:
And not to us, but to Thy arm alone,
Ascribe we all: when, without stratagem,
But in plain shock, and even play of battle,
Was ever known so great and little loss?
On one part and on th' other, take it God,
For it is none but Thine.

EXETER: 'Tis wonderful.

KING HENRY: Come, go we in procession to the village:
And be it death proclaimed through our host,
To boast of this, or take that praise from God,
Which is His only.

FLUELLEN: Is it not lawful and please your Majesty, to tell how many is kill'd?

KING HENRY: Yes Captain: but with this acknowledgement,
That God fought for us.

FLUELLEN: Yes, my conscience, He did us great good.

KING HENRY: Do we all holy rites:
Let there be sung *Non nobis* and *Te Deum*,
The dead with charity enclos'd in clay:
And then to Callice, and to England then,
Where ne'er from France arriv'd more happy men.

Exeunt.

V

Enter Chorus.

CHORUS: Vouchsafe to those that have not read the story,
That I may prompt them: and of such as have,
I humbly pray them to admit th'excuse

Of time, of numbers, and due course of things,
Which cannot in their huge and proper life,
Be here presented. Now we bear the King
Toward Callice: grant him there; there seen,
Heave him away upon your winged thoughts,
Athwart the sea: behold the English beach
Pales in the flood; with men, with wives, and boys,
Whose shouts and claps out-voice the deep-mouth'd sea,
Which like a mighty whiffler 'fore the King,
Seems to prepare his way: so let him land,
And solemnly see him set on to London.
So swift a pace hath thought, that even now
You may imagine him upon Blackheath:
Where, that his Lords desire him, to have borne
His bruised helmet, and his bended sword
Before him, through the City: he forbids it,
Being free from vainness, and self-glorious pride;
Giving full trophy, signal, and ostent,
Quite from himself, to God. But now behold.
In the quick forge and working-house of thought,
How London doth pour out her citizens,
The Mayor and all his brethren in best sort,
Like to the Senators of th' antique Rome,
With the plebeians swarming at their heels,
Go forth and fetch their conquering Cæsar in:
As by a lower, but by loving likelihood,
Were now the General of our gracious Empress,
As in good time he may, from Ireland coming,
Bringing rebellion broached on his sword;
How many would the peaceful City quit,
To welcome him? much more, and much more cause,
Did they this Harry. Now in London place him.
As yet the lamentation of the French

Invites the King of England's stay at home:
The Emperor's coming in behalf of France,
To order peace between them: and omit
All the occurrences, whatever chanc'd,
Till Harry's back return again to France:
There must we bring him; and myself have play'd
The interim, by remembering you 'tis past.
Then brook abridgement, and your eyes advance,
After your thoughts, straight back again to France.
Exit.

V.I

Enter Fluellen and Gower.

GOWER: Nay, that's right: but why wear you your leek to-day? Saint Davy's day is past.

FLUELLEN: There is occasions and causes why and wherefore in all things: I will tell you asse my friend, Captain Gower; the rascally, scauld, beggarly, lousy, pragging knave Pistol, which you and yourself, and all the World, know to be no petter than a fellow, look you now, of no merits: he is come to me, and prings me pread and salt yesterday, look you, and bid me eat my leek: it was in a place where I could not breed no contention with hi n; but I will be so bold as to wear it in my cap till I see him once again, and then I will tell him a little piece of my desires.

Enter Pistol.

GOWER: Why here he comes, swelling like a turkey-cock.

FLUELLEN: 'Tis no matter for his swellings, nor his turkey-cocks. God pless you Aunchient Pistol: you scurvy lousy knave, God pless you.

PISTOL: Ha, art thou bedlam? dost thou thirst, base Trojan,

to have me fold up Parca's fatal web? Hence; I am qualmish at the smell of leek.

FLUELLEN: I peseech you heartily, scurvy lousy knave, at my desires, and my requests, and my petitions, to eat, look you, this leek; because, look you, you do not love it, nor your affections, and your appetites and your digestions doo's not agree with it, I would desire you to eat it.

PISTOL: Not for Cadwallader and all his goats.

FLUELLEN: There is one goat for you.

Strikes him.

Will you be so good, scauld knave, as eat it?

PISTOL: Base Trojan, thou shalt die.

FLUELLEN: You say very true, scauld knave, when God's will is: I will desire you to live in the mean time, and eat your victuals: come, there is sauce for it. You call'd me yesterday mountain-squire, but I will make you to-day a squire of low degree. I pray you fall to, if you can mock a leek, you can eat a leek.

GOWER: Enough Captain, you have astonish'd him.

FLUELLEN: I say, I will make him eat some part of my leek, or I will peat his pate four days: bite I pray you, it is good for your green wound, and your ploody coxcomb.

PISTOL: Must I bite?

FLUELLEN: Yes certainly, and out of doubt and out of question too, and ambiguities.

PISTOL: By this leek, I will most horribly revenge: I eat and eat I swear.

FLUELLEN: Eat I pray you, will you have some more sauce to your leek: there is not enough leek to swear by.

PISTOL: Quiet thy cudgel, thou dost see I eat.

FLUELLEN: Much good do you scauld knave, heartily. Nay, pray you throw none away, the skin is good for your broken coxcomb; when you take occasions to see leeks hereafter, I pray you mock at 'em, that is all.

PISTOL: Good.

FLUELLEN: Ay, leeks is good: hold you, there is a groat to heal your pate.

PISTOL: Me a groat?

FLUELLEN: Yes verily, and in truth you shall take it, or I have another leek in my pocket, which you shall eat.

PISTOL: I take thy groat in earnest of revenge.

FLUELLEN: If I owe you any thing, I will pay you in cudgels, you shall be a woodmonger, and buy nothing of me but cudgels: God b' wi' you, and keep you, and heal your pate.

Exit.

PISTOL: All hell shall stir for this.

GOWER: Go, go, you are a counterfeit cowardly knave, will you mock at an ancient tradition began upon an honourable respect, and worn as a memorable trophy of predeceased valour, and dare not avouch in your deeds any of your words? I have seen you gleeking and galling at this gentleman twice or thrice. You thought, because he could not speak English in the native garb, he could not therefore handle an English cudgel: you find it otherwise, and henceforth let a Welsh correction, teach you a good English condition; fare ye well.

Exit.

PISTOL: Doth Fortune play the huswife with me now? News have I that my Doll is dead i' th' Spital of a malady of France, and there my rendezvous is quite cut off: old I do wax, and from my weary limbs honour is cudgell'd. Well, bawd I'll turn, and something lean to

cutpurse of quick hand: to England will I steal, and there I'll steal:
And patches will I get unto these cudgell'd scars,
And swear I got them in the Gallia wars.
Exit.

V.2

Enter at one door, King Henry, Exeter, Bedford, Warwick, and other Lords. At another, Queen Isabel, the French King, Katharine, Duke of Burgundy, and other French.

KING HENRY: Peace to this meeting, wherefore we are met;
Unto our brother France, and to our sister
Health and fair time of day: joy and good wishes
To our most fair and princely cousin Katharine:
And as a branch and member of this royalty,
By whom this great assembly is contriv'd,
We do salute you Duke of Burgundy,
And Princes French and Peers, health to you all.

FRENCH KING: Right joyous are we to behold your face,
Most worthy brother England, fairly met,
So are you, Princes (English) every one.

QUEEN ISABEL: So happy be the issue brother England,
Of this good day, and of this gracious meeting,
As we are now glad to behold your eyes,
Your eyes which hitherto have borne in them
Against the French that met them in their bent,
The fatal balls of murdering basilisks:
The venom of such looks we fairly hope
Have lost their quality, and that this day
Shall change all griefs and quarrels into love.

KING HENRY: To cry Amen to that, thus we appear.

QUEEN ISABEL: You English Princes all, I do salute you.
BURGUNDY: My duty to you both, on equal love.
Great Kings of France and England: that I have labour'd
With all my wits, my pains, and strong endeavours,
To bring your most Imperial Majesties
Unto this bar, and royal interview;
Your Mightiness on both parts best can witness.
Since then my office hath so far prevail'd,
That face to face, and royal eye to eye,
You have congreeted: let it not disgrace me,
If I demand before this royal view,
What rub, or what impediment there is,
Why that the naked, poor, and mangled Peace,
Dear nurse of arts, plenties, and joyful births,
Should not in this best garden of the World,
Our fertile France, put up her lovely visage?
Alas, she hath from France too long been chas'd,
And all her husbandry doth lie on heaps,
Corrupting in it own fertility.
Her vine, the merry cheerer of the heart,
Unpruned, dies: her hedges even pleach'd,
Like prisoners wildly over-grown with hair,
Put forth disorder'd twigs: her fallow leas,
The darnel, hemlock, and rank fumitory,
Doth root upon: while that the coulter rusts,
That should deracinate such savagery:
The even mead, that erst brought sweetly forth
The freckled cowslip, burnet, and green clover,
Wanting the scythe, all uncorrected, rank,
Conceives by idleness, and nothing teems,
But hateful docks, rough thistles, kecksies, burs,
Losing both beauty and utility;
And all our vineyards, fallows, meads and hedges,

Defective in their natures, grow to wildness.
Even so our houses, and ourselves, and children,
Have lost, or do not learn, for want of time,
The sciences that should become our country;
But grow like savages, as soldiers will,
That nothing do, but meditate on blood,
To swearing, and stern looks, defus'd attire,
And every thing that seems unnatural.
Which to reduce into our former favour,
You are assembled: and my speech entreats,
That I may know the let, why gentle Peace
Should not expel these inconveniences,
And bless us with her former qualities.

KING HENRY: If Duke of Burgundy, you would the peace,
Whose want gives growth to th' imperfections
Which you have cited; you must buy that peace
With full accord to all our just demands,
Whose tenours and particular effects
You have enschedul'd briefly in your hands.

BURGUNDY: The King hath heard them: to the which, as yet
There is no answer made.

KING HENRY: Well then: the peace which you before so urg'd,
Lies in his answer.

FRENCH KING: I have but with a cursorary eye
O'erglanc'd the articles: pleaseth your Grace
To appoint some of your Council presently
To sit with us once more, with better heed
To re-survey them; we will suddenly
Pass our accept and peremptory answer.

KING HENRY: Brother we shall. Go uncle Exeter,

And brother Clarence, and you brother Gloucester,
Warwick, and Huntingdon, go with the King,
And take with you free power, to ratify,
Augment, or alter, as your wisdoms best
Shall see advantageable for our dignity,
Any thing in or out of our demands,
And we'll consign thereto. Will you, fair sister,
Go with the Princes, or stay here with us?

QUEEN ISABEL: Our gracious brother, I will go with them:
Haply a woman's voice may do some good,
When articles too nicely urg'd, be stood on.

KING HENRY: Yet leave our cousin Katharine here with us:
She is our capital demand, compris'd
Within the fore-rank of our articles.

QUEEN ISABEL: She hath good leave.

Exeunt omnes. Manet King, and Katharine, and Lady.

KING HENRY: Fair Katharine, and most fair,
Will you vouchsafe to teach a soldier terms,
Such as will enter at a Lady's ear,
And plead his love-suit to her gentle heart?

KATHARINE: Your Majesty shall mock at me, I cannot speak your England.

KING HENRY: O fair Katharine, if you will love me soundly with your French heart, I will be glad to hear you confess it brokenly with your English tongue. Do you like me, Kate?

KATHARINE: *Pardonnez-moi,* I cannot tell vat is like me.

KING HENRY: An angel is like you Kate, and you are like an angel.

KATHARINE: *Que dit-il? que je suis semblable à les anges?*

ALICE: *Oui, vraiment (sauf votre grace) ainsi dit-il.*

KING HENRY: I said so, dear Katharine, and I must not blush to affirm it.

KATHARINE: *O bon Dieu, les langues des hommes sont pleines de tromperies.*

KING HENRY: What says she, fair one? that the tongues of men are full of deceits?

ALICE: *Oui,* dat de tongues of de mans is be full of deceits: dat is de Princess.

KING HENRY: The Princess is the better Englishwoman: i' faith Kate, my wooing is fit for thy understanding, I am glad thou canst speak no better English, for if thou couldst, thou wouldst find me such a plain King, that thou wouldst think, I had sold my farm to buy my crown. I know no ways to mince it in love, but directly to say, I love you; then if you urge me farther, than to say, Do you in faith? I wear out my suit: give me your answer, i' faith do, and so clap hands, and a bargain: how say you, Lady?

KATHARINE: *Sauf votre honneur,* me understand well.

KING HENRY: Marry, if you would put me to verses, or to dance for your sake, Kate, why you undid me: for the one I have neither words nor measure; and for the other, I have no strength in measure, yet a reasonable measure in strength. If I could win a Lady at leap-frog, or by vaulting into my saddle, with my armour on my back; under the correction of bragging be it spoken, I should quickly leap into a wife: or if I might buffet for my love, or bound my horse for her favours, I could lay on like a butcher, and sit like a Jack-an-apes, never off. But before God Kate, I cannot look greenly, nor gasp out my eloquence, nor I have no cunning in protestation; only downright oaths, which I never use till urg'd, nor never break for urging. If thou canst love a fellow of this temper, Kate, whose face is not worth sun-burning, that never looks in his glass, for love of any thing he sees there, let thine eye be thy cook. I speak to thee plain soldier: if thou canst love me for this, take me; if not, to say to thee that I shall die, is true; but for thy love, by the Lord no: yet I love thee too. And while thou liv'st, dear Kate, take a fellow of plain and uncoined constancy, for he perforce must do thee right, because he hath not the gift to woo in other places: for these fellows of infinite tongue, that can rhyme themselves into Ladies' favours, they do always reason themselves out again. What? a speaker is but a prater, a rhyme is but a ballad; a good leg will fall, a straight back will stoop, a black beard will turn white, a curl'd pate will grow bald, a fair face will wither, a full eye will wax hollow: but a good heart, Kate, is the sun and the moon, or rather the sun, and not the moon; for it shines bright, and never changes, but keeps his course truly. If thou would have such a one, take me; and take me; take a soldier: take a soldier; take a King. And what sayest thou then to my love? speak my fair, and fairly, I pray thee.

KATHARINE: Is it possible dat I sould love de enemy of France?

KING HENRY: No, it is not possible you should love the enemy of France, Kate; but in loving me, you should love the friend of France: for I love France so well, that I will not part with a village of it; I will have it all mine: and Kate, when France is mine, and I am yours; then yours is France, and you are mine.

KATHARINE: I cannot tell wat is dat.

KING HENRY: No, Kate? I will tell thee in French, which I am sure will hang upon my tongue, like a new-married wife about her husband's neck, hardly to be shook off; *Je quand sur le possession de France, et quand vous avez le possession de moi* (let me see, what then? Saint Denis be my speed) *donc votre est France, et vous êtes mienne.* It is as easy for me, Kate, to conquer the Kingdom, as to speak so much more French: I shall never move thee in French, unless it be to laugh at me.

KATHARINE: *Sauf votre honneur, le François que vous parlez, il est meilleur que l'Anglois lequel je parle.*

KING HENRY: No faith is't not, Kate: but thy speaking of my tongue, and I thine, most truly falsely, must needs be granted to be much at one. But Kate, dost thou understand thus much English? Canst thou love me?

KATHARINE: I cannot tell.

KING HENRY: Can any of your neighbours tell, Kate? I'll ask them. Come, I know thou lovest me: and at night, when you come into your closet, you'll question this gentlewoman about me; and I know, Kate, you will to her dispraise those parts in me, that you love with your heart: but good Kate, mock me mercifully, the rather gentle Princess, because I love thee cruelly. If ever thou beest mine, Kate, as I have a saving faith within me tells me thou shalt, I get thee with scambling, and thou must therefore needs prove a good soldier-breeder: shall not thou and I, between Saint Denis and Saint George, compound a boy, half French half English, that shall go to Constantinople, and take the Turk by the beard? Shall we not? what say'st thou, my fair flower-de-luce?

KATHARINE: I do not know dat.

KING HENRY: No: 'tis hereafter to know, but now to promise: do but now promise Kate, you will endeavour for your French part of such a boy; and for my English moiety, take the word of a King, and a bachelor. How answer you, *la plus belle Katharine du monde, mon très cher et devin déesse?*

KATHARINE: Your Majestee ave fause French enough to deceive de most sage Demoiselle dat is en France.

KING HENRY: Now fie upon my false French: by mine honour in true English, I love thee Kate: by which honour, I dare not swear thou lovest me, yet my blood begins to flatter me, that thou dost; notwithstanding the poor and untempering effect of my visage. Now beshrew my father's ambition, he was thinking of civil wars when he got me, therefore was I created with a stubborn outside, with an aspect of iron, that when I come to woo ladies, I fright them: but in faith Kate, the elder I wax, the better I shall appear. My comfort is, that old age, that ill layer up of beauty, can do no more spoil upon my face. Thou hast me, if thou hast me, at the worst; and thou shalt wear me, if thou wear me, better and better: and therefore tell me, most fair Katharine, will you have me? Put off your maiden blushes, avouch the thoughts of your heart with the looks of an Empress, take me by the hand, and say, Harry of England, I am thine: which word thou shalt no sooner bless mine ear withal, but I will tell thee aloud, England is thine, Ireland is thine, France is thine, and Henry Plantagenet is thine; who, though I speak it before his face, if he be not fellow with the best King, thou shalt find the best King of good fellows. Come your answer in broken music; for thy voice is music, and thy English broken: therefore Queen of all, Katharine, break thy mind to me in broken English; wilt thou have me?

KATHARINE: Dat is as it shall please *de Roi mon père.*

KING HENRY: Nay, it will please him well, Kate; it shall please him, Kate.

KATHARINE: Den it sall also content me.

KING HENRY: Upon that I kiss your hand, and I call you my Queen.

KATHARINE: *Laissez mon Seigneur, laissez, laissez, ma foi: je ne veux point que vous abaissiez votre grandeur, en baisant la main d'une de votre Seigneurie indigne serviteur; excusez-moi, je vous supplie, mon très-puissant Seigneur.*

KING HENRY: Then I will kiss your lips, Kate.

KATHARINE: *Les Dames et Demoiselles pour être baisées devant leur noces, il n'est pas la coutume de France.*

KING HENRY: Madam, my interpreter, what says she?

ALICE: Dat it is not be de fashon pour les Ladies of France; I cannot tell vat is baiser en Anglish.

KING HENRY: To kiss.

ALICE: Your Majesty *entendre bettre que moi.*

KING HENRY: It is not a fashion for the maids in France to kiss before they are married, would she say?

ALICE: *Oui vraiment.*

KING HENRY: O Kate, nice customs curtsy to great Kings. Dear Kate, you and I cannot be confin'd within the weak list of a country's fashion: we are the makers of manners, Kate; and the liberty that follows our places, stops the mouth of all find-faults, as I will do yours, for upholding the nice fashion of your country, in denying me a kiss: therefore patiently, and yielding. You have witchcraft in your lips, Kate: there is more eloquence in a sugar touch of them, than in the tongues of the French Council; and they should sooner persuade Harry of England, than a general petition of Monarchs. Here comes your father.

Enter the French King and Queen and Lords, and the English Lords.

BURGUNDY: God save your Majesty, my Royal Cousin, teach you our Princess English?

KING HENRY: I would have her learn, my fair Cousin, how perfectly I love her, and that is good English.

BURGUNDY: Is she not apt?

KING HENRY: Our tongue is rough, coz, and my condition is not smooth: so that having neither the voice nor the heart of flattery about me, I cannot so conjure up the Spirit of Love in her, that he will appear in his true likeness.

BURGUNDY: Pardon the frankness of my mirth, if I answer you for that. If you would conjure in her, you must make a circle: if conjure up Love in her in his true likeness, he must appear naked, and blind. Can you blame her then, being a maid, yet ros'd over with the virgin crimson of modesty, if she deny the appearance of a naked blind boy in her naked seeing self? It were (my Lord) a hard condition for a maid to consign to.

KING HENRY: Yet they do wink and yield, as love is blind and enforces.

BURGUNDY: They are then excus'd, my Lord, when they see not what they do.

KING HENRY: Then good my Lord, teach your cousin to consent winking.

BURGUNDY: I will wink on her to consent, my Lord, if you will teach her to know my meaning: for maids well summer'd and warm kept, are like flies at Bartholomew-tide, blind, though they have their eyes, and then they will endure handling, which before would not abide looking on.

KING HENRY: This moral ties me over to time, and a hot summer; and so I shall catch the fly, your cousin, in the latter end, and she must be blind too.

BURGUNDY: As Love is my Lord, before it loves.

KING HENRY: It is so: and you may, some of you, thank Love for my blindness, who cannot see many a fair French city for one fair French maid that stands in my way.

FRENCH KING: Yes my Lord, you see them perspectively: the cities turn'd into a maid; for they are all girdled with maiden walls, that war hath never entered.

KING HENRY: Shall Kate be my wife?

FRENCH KING: So please you.

KING HENRY: I am content, so the maiden cities you talk of, may wait on her: so the maid that stood in the way for my wish, shall show me the way to my will.

FRENCH KING: We have consented to all terms of reason.

KING HENRY: Is't so, my Lords of England?

WESTMORELAND: The King hath granted every article:
His daughter first; and then in sequel, all,
According to their firm proposed natures.

EXETER: Only he hath not yet subscribed this: Where your Majesty demands, That the King of France, having any occasion to write for matter of grant, shall name your Highness in this form, and with this addition, in French: *Notre très-cher fils Henri Roi d'Angleterre Héritier de France;* and thus in Latin, *Præclarissimus filius noster Henricus Rex Angliæ et Hæres Franciæ.*

FRENCH KING: Nor this I have not brother so deni'd,
But your request shall make me let it pass.

KING HENRY: I pray you then, in love and dear alliance,
Let that one article rank with the rest,
And thereupon give me your daughter.

FRENCH KING: Take her fair son, and from her blood raise up
Issue to me, that the contending Kingdoms

Of France and England, whose very shores look pale,
With envy of each other's happiness,
May cease their hatred; and this dear conjunction
Plant neighbourhood and Christian-like accord
In their sweet bosoms: that never war advance
His bleeding sword 'twixt England and fair France.

LORDS: Amen.

KING HENRY: Now welcome Kate: and bear me witness all,
That here I kiss her as my Sovereign Queen.

Flourish.

QUEEN ISABEL: God, the best maker of all marriages,
Combine your hearts in one, your Realms in one:
As man and wife being two, are one in love,
So be there 'twixt your Kingdoms such a spousal,
That never may ill office, or fell jealousy,
Which troubles oft the bed of blessed marriage,
Thrust in between the paction of these kingdoms,
To make divorce of their incorporate league;
That English may as French, French Englishmen,
Receive each other. God speak this Amen.

ALL: Amen.

KING HENRY: Prepare we for our marriage: on which day,
My Lord of Burgundy we'll take your oath
And all the Peers', for surety of our leagues.
Then shall I swear to Kate, and you to me,
And may our oaths well kept and prosperous be.

Sennet.

Exeunt.

Enter Chorus.

CHORUS: Thus far with rough, and all-unable pen,
Our bending author hath pursu'd the story,

In little room confining mighty men,
Mangling by starts the full course of their glory.
Small time: but in that small, most greatly lived
This Star of England. Fortune made his sword;
By which the World's best garden he achieved:
And of it left his son Imperial Lord.
Henry the Sixth, in infant bands crown'd King
Of France and England, did this King succeed:
Whose state so many had the managing,
That they lost France, and made his England bleed:
Which oft our stage hath shown; and for their sake,
In your fair minds let this acceptance take.

FINIS

NOTES

References are to the page and line of this edition; the full page contains 33 lines.

P. 23 — *Enter Prologue:* Shakespeare seldom introduces a Prologue or Chorus to address the audience. This appeal to the spectators to use their imaginations answers the criticisms of Ben Jonson who sneered at the players for attempting to present history with the help of 'three rusty swords'.

P. 23 L. 4 — *Heaven of invention:* utmost height of inspiration.

P. 23 L. 15 — *this wooden O:* the small Curtain playhouse which the company were using until their new playhouse, the Globe, was ready. In the Christmas holidays of 1598, the players, with the aid of a builder and his workmen, demolished the old Theatre and removed the timbers to a site already prepared in Southwark. Until the new house was ready, they acted in the Curtain in Shoreditch.

P. 23 L. 20 — *imaginary forces:* power of imagination.

P. 25 L. 5 — *The courses of his youth:* The wildness of the King as a young man, and his sudden reformation are shown in the first and second parts of *Henry the Fourth.*

P. 25 L. 9 — *Consideration:* serious thoughtfulness.

P. 25 L. 10 — *offending Adam:* i.e., original sin.

P. 25 L. 30 — *charter'd libertine:* a free thing imprisoned.

P. 25 L. 33 — *art ... theoric:* his theories of life must be founded on his practical experience.

P. 26 L. 15 — *crescive ... faculty:* growing by its own natural power.

P. 28 L. 5 — *the Law Salique:* The Salic Law prohibited the succession of females, as explained later by the Archbishop.

P. 28 L. 10 — *opening titles miscreate:* making claims falsely based.

There is no bar. ...: The whole of this long argument is a very close paraphrase from Holinshed. P. 28 L. 30

Book of Numbers: Chapter xxvii, verse 8. 'And thou shalt speak unto the children of Israel, saying, If a man die, and have no son, then ye shall cause his inheritance to pass unto his daughter.' P. 30 L. 28

great-grandsire: i.e. Edward the Third. P. 30 L. 33

play'd a tragedy: The reference is to the Battle of Crecy, 1346. P. 31 L. 3

pilfering Borderers: There was a constant state of war along the English and Scottish Border, throughout the Middle Ages, and in Shakespeare's time. P. 32 L. 8

coursing snatchers: raiding thieves. P. 32 L. 9

The King of Scots ... send to France: This is not accurate. King David II was taken prisoner at Nevill's Cross in 1346, but he remained in England. P. 32 L. 29

tear: for Folio reading 'tame'. P. 33 L. 7

for so work the honey-bees: The parable of a Kingdom compared with a bee-hive is not uncommon. John Lyly in *Euphues and his England* (edited by R. Warwick Bond, ii, 44–5) worked it out elaborately. In the Parliament of 1593 the Speaker in his speech before the Queen remarked, 'I must presume to say that which hath often been said: this secret counsel of ours I would compare to the sweet commonwealth of the little bees.' Neither Shakespeare nor the others show more than a poetic knowledge of bee-hives. P. 33 L. 22

End in: for Folio 'And'. P. 34 L. 14

waxen epitaph: a memorial soon obliterated. Shakespeare is probably referring to the custom of carrying an effigy of wax in the funeral processions of Kings, which was set up on the tomb until the permanent memorial was erected. Several of these effigies still survive in Westminster Abbey. P. 35 L. 3

cousin Dolphin: Although editors usually alter the word to 'Dauphin', Shakespeare and his contemporaries called him 'the Dolphin'. There is no point in translating it. P. 35 L. 6

P. 35 L. 9 *Freely... charge:* An Ambassador who too freely expressed the mind of his master ran some risks, as the Polish Ambassador found when he delivered his message overfrankly to Queen Elizabeth on 23rd July, 1597.

P. 35 L. 24 *galliard:* a lively dance, suitable for the young.

P. 35 L. 31 *Tennis balls:* made of leather stuffed with hair. Elizabethan tennis was an elaborate form of the modern rackets.

'The court is an enclosed oblong building, having on one side and at the two ends an inner wall between which and the outer wall is a sloping roof, the 'penthouse'. Pericles, when tossed by the rackety waves, speaks of himself as

A man whom both the waters and the wind,
In that vast tennis-court (the sea), have made the ball
For them to play upon. (*Pericles* II. i. 64–6.)

In the inner wall are openings, called hazards, such as the *trou*, or hole near the floor, and later, galleries. The chase is the second impact on the floor (or in a gallery) of a ball which the opponent has failed or declined to return; its value is determined by the nearness of the point of impact to the end wall. A chase does not count to either player until the players have changed sides. A player wins a chase, on sides being changed, if he can cause his ball to rebound nearer the wall than the ball did in the chase for which he is playing.'

(*Shakespeare's England ii*, 460.)

P. 37 L. 25 *silken dalliance:* silk clothes, suitable for flirtation.

P. 38 L. 24 *digest ... distance:* 'overcome the difficulties of place.'

P. 38 L. 25 *force a play:* make historical events fit into our play.

P. 39 L. 5 *Lieutenant Bardolph:* This worthy has been promoted. He was only a corporal in *II Henry IV*.

P. 39 L. 8 *Ancient:* Ensign, the junior officer in the company who carried the company colours.

P. 39 L. 20 *rendezvous:* perhaps 'last resort', but Nym's use of words is peculiar.

troth-plight: betrothed. Betrothal was a formal promise to marry made verbally before witnesses – and was legally binding. Elizabethan legal records abound in the wrangles arising from an arrangement so easily abused. P. 39 L. 23

mare: for Folio reading 'name'. P. 39 L. 27

call'st ... host: Pistol, by his marriage with Mistress Quickly, has taken over her tavern, but as a soldier he scorns to be considered a tradesman. P. 40 L. 1

drawn: for Folio reading 'hewn'. P. 40 L. 8

prickear'd ... Iceland: Iceland dogs were shaggy and quarrelsome. P. 40 L. 13

prickear'd: with straight erect ears. P. 40 L. 13

and that's the humour of it: The word humour was at this time much in the mouths of the would-be intellectuals, to denote an idiosyncrasy or oddity of behaviour. Ben Jonson in *Every Man out of his Humour* (written about the same time as Henry V) lectured at length on the misuse of the word. Nym and Pistol, in their vocabularies, parody two types of stage jargon; the disreputable Nym echoes the intellectual; Pistol models his general behaviour and diction on the old-fashioned barnstorming ways still in vogue at the rival playhouse, the Rose, where Edward Alleyne, the tragic actor, had made his name in such furious and bombastic parts as Tamburlaine, Orlando Furioso, Dr Faustus and the Jew of Malta. Most of Pistol's more furious remarks are misquotations from plays which were being acted at the Rose. P. 40 L. 28

exhale: draw your last breath. P. 40 L. 32

Couple a gorge: Elizabethan soldiers' French for 'Cut his throat'. P. 41 L. 8

powdering-tub: sweating tub, used in the cure of venereal disease. P. 41 L. 10

lazar kite of Cressid's kind: lazars, beggars (lit., lepers like Lazarus in the parable) like Cressida, the Trojan strumpet. Doll Tearsheet is the prostitute, attached to the inn kept by Mistress Quickly (now Mistress Pistol) in *II Henry IV*. P. 41 L. 11

P. 41 L. 16 *my master:* i.e. Sir John Falstaff. At the end of *II Henry IV*, Shakespeare promised to continue Falstaff, but he did not. Perhaps he had lost the knack of Falstaff (and certainly in *The Merry Wives* Falstaff is woefully abated); possibly the actor who took the part had gone.

P. 41 L. 19 *office of a warming-pan:* The warming pan was a copper pan, with a lid, filled with hot coal, used to warm a bed. Bardolph has a face and nose of fiery redness; see p. 50, l 15.

P. 41 L. 21 *crow ... pudding:* be hanged and devoured by the crows,

P. 42 L. 8 *A noble:* i. e. 6*s.* 8*d.* – a reduction for ready cash.

P. 42 L. 19 *quotidian tertian:* Mrs. Quickly is always a little mixed in her talk, especially when she uses the long words. A 'quotidian' is a fever recurring daily, a 'tertian' a fever recurring every third day.

P. 46 L. 20 *All other devils ... piety:* 'Those devils which prompt men to commit treason persuaded them that it is a godly action.'

P. 47 L. 12 *To mark:* for Folio reading 'make'.

P. 49 L. 16 *Arthur's bosom:* Mrs Quickly means Abraham's bosom, whence Lazarus in the parable looked down on Dives in torment.

P. 49 L. 18 *christom child:* a child in its christening robe, an innocent.

P. 49 L. 22 *and a' talk of green fields:* The Folio reads, 'and a Table of greene fields'. Theobald in 1726 emended 'a Table' to 'a' babbled' – the most famous of all Shakespearian emendations. It is, however, probably wrong. '*Table*' is a more likely misprinting of '*talke*' than of '*babled*', and, moreover, the passage in the Quarto reads – 'His nose was as sharp as a pen: for when I saw him fumble with the Sheets, and talk of floures. ...' In my own proofs, I have thrice met the misprint '*table*' for '*talk*' (or vice-versa).

P. 50 L. 6 *carnation:* flesh colour.

P. 50 L. 21 *the word is, pitch and pay:* pay on the nail – no running up of accounts. The Folio reads 'world'.

caveto: Pistolese for 'Caution'. P. 50 L. 23

How modest in exception: how modestly he differs from his advisers. P. 52 L. 9

Roman Brutus: Lucius Junius Brutus, ancestor of that Brutus who slew Julius Caesar, drove Tarquin the tyrant away from Rome. To avoid suspicion he pretended to be a half-wit. P. 52 L. 12

pining: for Folio reading 'privy'. P. 54 L. 22

Hampton: the Folio reads 'Dover'. P. 56 L. 6

Grapple your minds to sternage: 'Follow in imagination the sterns.' P. 56 L. 20

summon: For Folio reading 'Commune'. P. 57 L. 19

Callice: the Folio spelling, reproducing the usual pronunciation of 'Calais', spelt also in Shakespeare's time 'Calis'. P. 59 L. 28

carry coals: do any dirty work. P. 59 L. 29

precepts to the leviathan: commands to the whale. P. 63 L. 21

Act III, Scene 4: About 1602–4 Shakespeare was lodging in London with a Huguenot family named Mountjoy and took some interest in the affairs of Mary Mountjoy, the daughter of the house. Some commentators please themselves with the fancy that she taught Shakespeare enough French for the scene. Actually the purpose of this episode is to get some low amusement from the fact that certain word-sounds, innocent in one language, are bawdy in another. The Folio printer made a sad mess of the French, which is here restored following the usual practice of editors. P. 64

nook-shotten: containing many nooks, i.e. with a coast full of inlets. P. 67 L. 4

lavoltas high, and swift corantos: Sir John Davies in *Orchestra or a poem of Dancing*, describes the Coranto: P. 67 L. 24

> What shall I name those current traverses,
> That on a triple *dactile* foot do run
> Close by the ground with sliding passages,

Wherein that dancer greatest praise hath won
Which with best order can all order shun;
For everywhere he wantonly must range,
And turn, and wind, with unexpected change.

And the Lavolta:

Yet there is one, the most delightful kind,
A lofty jumping, or a leaping round;
Where arm in arm two dancers are entwined
And whirl themselves with strict embracements bound
And still their feet an *anapest* do sound;
And *anapest* is all their music's song,
Whose first two feet are short, and third is long.
(Stanzas 69, 70.)

P. 67 L. 32 *Charles Delabreth ... Charolois:* These names were taken direct from Holinshed.

P. 68 L. 11 *void his rheum:* spit.

P. 68 L. 13 *Roan:* the normal Elizabethan spelling of Rouen.

P. 70 L. 13 *pax of little price:* Either Shakespeare or his printer has misread Holinshed who tells how a soldier was hanged for stealing a 'pyx'. The pyx is a vessel for holding the Consecrated Host; the pax was a plate, stamped with a figure of the crucifix, kissed first by the priest and then by the congregation.

P. 70 L. 25 *figo ... the fig of Spain:* a lewd and expressive gesture of immemorial antiquity, made by putting the thumb between two fingers. As a boy I have seen the gesture made at an Italian organ-grinder with gratifying results.

P. 71 L. 12 *beard of the General's cut:* During the Cadiz voyage of 1596, the Earl of Essex grew a large beard. Many of his followers imitated the fashion which was known as the 'Cadiz beard'.

P. 74 L. 28 *pasterns:* the Folio reads 'postures'.

P. 74 L. 30 *When I bestride him, I soar:* The French were noted for their skill in horsemanship.

P. 76 L. 2 *kern of Ireland ... strait strossers:* Strossers are underpants, but the wild Irish soldiers were said to go in 'strait strossers' because, by reason of the bogs wherein they lurked, they wore nothing on their limbs.

la truie ... bourbier: the washed sow to her mire. P. 76 L. 13

hooded valour ... will bate: i.e. like a hawk when the hood is removed, it will flap its wings. P. 77 L. 26

mastiffs ... rotten apples: Mastiffs were bred and trained for bear baiting. P. 78 L. 24

entertain conjecture: imagine. P. 79 L. 11

low-rated ... dice: gamble for the ransoms of the English when they shall be taken, for what little they may be worth. Gentlemen who followed the wars hoped to make a handsome profit from the ransoms of their prisoners which belonged to their captors. P. 79 L. 29

over-bears attaint: overcomes the taint of fear. P. 80 L. 18

four ... ragged foils: The Elizabethan players had few supers at their disposal for their crowd and battle scenes. See note on p. 23. P. 80 L. 29

gentleman of a company: i.e. a volunteer, and not (as were the majority of Elizabethan soldiers) a pressed man. Gentlemen volunteers who served as infantry were usually pikemen. P. 82 L. 16

speak fewer: often amended to 'speak lower'. Fluellen would have no talking after lights-out, but is an arrant chatterbox himself. P. 83 L. 11

But if the cause be not good. ...: Anyone who has served with soldiers will recognize that perennial type the 'company lawyer'. P. 85 L. 14

proportion of subjection: proper behaviour of a subject. P. 85 L. 25

an elder-gun: pop-gun made of elder wood – a harmless weapon. P. 87 L. 11

the fault My father made. The theme of the whole cycle of the History plays from *Richard II* to *Richard III* is that by usurping the crown of Richard II, Henry IV brought a curse upon his House and the Kingdom. P. 90 L. 10

curtle-axe: cutlass, the weapon of a cavalryman which he used when his lance was splintered. P. 91 L. 28

P. 92 L. 26 *gimmal bit ... motionless: Gimmal* (emendation for the Folio spelling iymold i.e. jymold): jointed. The horses are in such poor condition that they are too jaded even to chew the grass.

P. 92 L. 28 *executors ... crows:* the crows who will succeed to what is left when they are dead.

P. 94 L. 27 *Crispian:* Crispin and Crispian were two brothers martyred at Soissons in 287 A.D., and the patron saints of shoemakers. Their day is 25th October.

P. 96 L. 29 *reeking up:* rising like mist.

P. 97 L. 2 *relapse of mortality:* with renewed deadliness.

P. 97 L. 7 *piece of feather:* the Elizabethan officer used to adorn his helmet with plumes of feathers, but Henry's army is now too bedraggled for any finery.

P. 98 IV. 4: In this scene also the French has been restored to sense by the editors.

P. 98 L. 7 *Qualtitie calmie custure me:* Pistolese French, of which the meaning is irrecoverable.

P. 98 L. 16 *rim:* actually the diaphragm, but Pistol simply means 'guts'.

P. 98 L. 28 *fer ... firk ... ferret:* 'give him fer'. *Firk,* beat, but 'Mr Stevens justly observed that this word is so licentiously used that it is not easy to fix its meaning' [Nares' *Glossary*] – like similar words which modern soldiers use. *Ferret:* to worry like a ferret.

P. 99 L. 5 *Owy, cuppele gorge permafoy:* Elizabethan soldiers served in France continuously between 1589 and 1597, and had their own versions of French phrases, such as *cuppele gorge or permafoy.* Their descendants in 1914–18 similarly had their own pronunciations, such as 'san fairy ann' or 'napoo'.

P. 100 L. 4 *roaring devil i' th' old play:* The devil in the old Miracle Plays was a popular character. He carried a wooden dagger and leapt about roaring.

P. 104 L. 4 *great-belly doublet:* 'The doublet ... was a closely fitting garment with detachable sleeves. ...' The great-belly doublet was a garment 'long in front, overhanging the girdle like the end of a peas-cod'.

[M. C. Linthicum, *Costume in the Drama of Shakespeare and his Contemporaries*, pp. 197–8].

book our dead: the Folio reads 'look'. P. 104 L. 33

to wear the leek: The true origin of the custom of wearing leeks on St. David's Day appears to be unknown. P. 105 L. 31

number ... English dead: The English losses have been variously estimated from 100 to 600 killed. The French lost 10,000 killed through their foolish tactics of charging in full armour over boggy ground against archers protected by a palisade of sharpened stakes. Incidentally, Shakespeare omits to mention the English archers. P. 111 L. 30

whiffler: the officer who makes a way through the crowd for a procession. P. 113 L. 9

the General of our gracious Empress ... from Ireland coming: On 27th March, 1599, the Earl of Essex set out from London for Ireland where he was to command a large army to put down the rebellion. Everywhere as he passed 'the people pressed exceedingly to behold him, especially in the highways for more than four miles space, crying and singing, "God bless your Lordship", "God preserve your Honour" etc. and some followed him till the evening, only to behold him' [John Stow's *Annals*]. Essex failed miserably, and his return in the autumn was less spectacular though more dramatic. This clear reference shows that the play was put on in the spring of 1599. P. 113 L. 27

my Doll: presumably Pistol meant Nell, though he might also have called her Doll, which was equivalent to the modern 'dearie'. P. 116 L. 30

basilisk: the largest of cannon. The basilisk, from which it took its name, was a very fabulous creature, bred from a cock's egg hatched by a serpent, and fatal to all that came near it. P. 117 L. 27

Our fertile France ... unnatural: This vivid description of a country wasted by war comes from someone's direct experience. It is not impossible that P. 118 L. 16

Shakespeare had himself seen war; his knowledge of soldiers and soldiering is unusually acute and detailed especially in those little matters which are beyond the imagination of a man of letters, or even a journalist interviewing a returned soldier. The desolation of France during the Civil Wars of the 1590's was much noted by those who rode with the Earl of Essex to Noyon in 1591.

P. 123 L. 25 *compound a boy.* ... Unfortunately the boy who became King Henry VI as a baby inherited the mental weakness of his French grandfather.

P. 123 L. 26 *go to Constantinople ... beard:* i.e. perform romantic and heroical exploits.

P. 126 L. 27 *flies at Bartholomew tide:* St. Bartholomew's Day is 24th August. Towards the end of summer flies grow torpid and are more easily caught.

P. 129 L. 11 *Which oft our stage hath shown:* i.e. in the three parts of *Henry VI*, of which the first part especially had been a most popular and successful play.

GLOSSARY

a': he
abutting: neighbouring
accomplish: prepare for battle
accompt: reckoning
achieve: slay
achievement: thing achieved, victory
admiration: astonishment
address'd: ready
advice: consideration
affiance: confidence
annoy: hurt
antics: buffoons
arbitrement: decision
attaint: infection (of fear)

bar: court
Barbason: the name of a fiend
battle: army
bawcock: *beau coq*, fine fellow
beaver: lower part of the face guard of a helmet
bedlam: madman.
bending: bowing
bolted: sifted
book: make a record of
boot: plunder
bootless: vain
bound: make prance
bow: bend, force
broached: impaled
broken music: music divided among various instruments
brook abridgment: excuse the omission
bubukles: carbuncles
buxom: lively

carnation: flesh-coloured
casques: helmets
case: set
chace: stroke in tennis
choler: wrath
close: cadence
companies: companions
compound: come to terms
complement: outward behaviour of a gentleman
confounded: pounded, worn
congreeing: agreeing
conjuration: solemn appeal
consent: harmony
consign: agree
convey'd: misrepresented
coranto: lively dance.
coursing snatchers: raiding bandits
crescive: growing
crouch: ready to spring.
crush'd: strained
crystals: eyes
cullions: rascals
currance: current
curtains: colours, flags

decoct: kindle
defunction: death
defus'd: disordered
deracinate: root out
despite: malice

dout: put out
down-roping: hanging down in strings

earn: grieve
earnest: payment on account
element: sky
empery: rule
enscheduled: listed
even-pleached: thick and even
executors: executioners

farced: stuffed out
fear'd: frightened
fet: fetched
fin'd: agreed to pay as a fine
flesh'd: tasted first blood
fox: sword
French hose: baggy breeches
fret: plunge wildly
full-fraught: full and perfect

gage: pledged
galled: worn by the tides
galliard: lively dance
giddy: unreliable
gleeking: mocking
glose: explain
gulf: whirlpool
gun-stones: cannon balls.

haggled: hacked
half-achieved: half won
hard-favour'd: grim
hazard: hole in the wall in tennis court
hilding: worthless
honour-owing: honourable
housewifery: careful management
huswife: hussy
Hyperion: the sun god

ill-favouredly: uglily
imaginary forces: power of imagination
imbar: bar in, defend
impawn: pledge
impeachment: hindrance
impounded: shut up in a pound
indifferent: impartial
intertissued: interwoven

Jack-a-napes: ape
Jacksauce: saucy fellow
jade: bad-tempered nag
jealousy: suspicion
jutty: jut over

larding: making fat, enriching
latest: last
lazars: beggars
legerity: nimbleness
likes: pleases
line: pedigree
linstock: gunner's match
list: boundary
luxury: list

Marches: Borders
maw: stomach
miscreate: spurious
moiety: part
mountain-squire: poor Welshman

native: natural
nicely: precisely

o'erwhelm: overhang
ordinance: cannon
ordure: manure

orisons: prayers
ostent: display
owing: possessing

paction: agreement
pales: fences
paly: pale
Parca: Fate
parle: parley
passing: exceedingly
pauca: few words
pavillion'd: in tents
Pegasus: the winged horse of Perseus
perspectively: distortedly
Phoebus: the sungod
pioners: sappers and miners
plain-song: ditty
poring: peering
port: bearing
portage: bearing
practices: treasons
present: immediate
pristine: antique
projection: expenditure
purchase: thieves' language for 'plunder'
purg'd judgment: impartial

quality: profession
quit: acquit
quittance: payment

raught: reached
raw: poorly provided
rest: determination
rheum: mist moisture
rivage: shore
rub: impediment

sack: dry Spanish wine, sherry, to which the late Sir John Falstaff was particularly partial.
scambling: shoving
scauld: scabby
scions: shoots used in grafting
secure: lack of care
security: carelessness
self: same
severals: particulars
sequestration: separation
shales: shells
shog off: move off
shrewdly: grievously
sinister: crooked
slip: dog collar for quick release
skirr: scurry
slobbery: sloppy
slough: skin
spend their mouths: bark
spittal: hospital
stoop: swoop
sumless: innumerable
sur-rein'd: over-ridden
sutler: canteen man
swashers: swashbucklers

Tartar: hell
temporal: originally belonging to the laity
threaden: woven
tucket-sonance: warning trumpet call
tun: barrel

umber'd: umber-coloured by the firelight
uncoined: genuine

ungotten: unbegotten

vaward: vanguard

winding up: completing
wrangler: opponent

wringing: pain

yearn: grieve
yeomen: farmers' sons
yerk: thrust